A BOND OF FIRE AND ROSES

A Bond of Fire and Roses

Roses

CROWNED BY WINGS SERIES

G. BAILEY

SCARLETT SNOW

❀ Created with Vellum

CONTENTS

Description   ix

Chapter 1   1
Chapter 2   31
Chapter 3   42
Chapter 4   67
Chapter 5   87
Chapter 6   102
Chapter 7   133
Chapter 8   155
Chapter 9   177
Chapter 10   201
Chapter 11   224
Chapter 12   234
Chapter 13   256
Chapter 14   276
Chapter 15   291
Chapter 16   303
Chapter 17   317

About the Author   331
About the Author   333
Shadowborn Academy bonus
read...   335

DESCRIPTION

**The dragon rider might have taken
everything from me.
My home, my family, and my crown.
But I vowed long ago he would never take
my heart.**

I survived ten years being tortured by his
crazy worshippers. I know I can survive
anything the king throws at me.
Because if this usurper thinks I'm going to
bend and break to his will now that I'm his
wife, he doesn't know what his new queen is
capable of.
I will make him bend and break.

I might not be a dragon rider like him, but I have dragon blood in my veins from an ancient bond forged by my ancestors, and its fire is fueled by the hatred I hold just for him. A hatred that burns.

~

I should have killed the princess when I burned her world to ash.

It was the least she deserved after what her parents did that day. But my own stubborn dragon refused to destroy the one person the gods decided was fated to me.

For years I have ignored her existence and tried to forget her screams. For years I 've tried to hate her and burn her memory from my mind, but now the time has come to claim my wife...

And make her my queen.

Crowned by Wings is a new romantasy series that features an explosive enemies-to-lovers romance that will either unite their warring kingdoms or burn them to the ground. The series contains dragon riders, magic, and explicit on page heat. Tropes: arranged marriage, enemies-to-lovers, touch-her-and-die, who did this to you.

CHAPTER ONE

"Wake up, Princess!"

Fire and smoke fill the air around me, smothering the pretty roses that sit on the table by my bed. The smoke burns the back of my throat as I cough and look up at Dasinth. His face is covered in shadows and my family's gold moon crest gleams on his red helmet and chestplate. Panic grips me. Dasinth is the captain of my father's guard and his most trusted advisor.

Why is he in my room?

"We must hurry if you wish to live," he whispers, pulling me from my bed by the arm. "Come quickly!"

I'm too shocked to make a noise. My guards are not allowed to touch me, let alone enter my chamber, unless my life is in danger. Not even

Dasinth, who is more like an uncle to me than a guard, has entered my room before. He throws a red dressing gown over my small shoulders and a pair of fur-lined slippers onto my feet. Briefly his eyes meet mine, and I see something in them that makes me tremble.

Fear.

"Where are we going, Dasinth? Where is Mama and Papa?"

"You must follow and keep quiet, Princess." He drags me outside into a corridor filled with thick black smoke. Screams and cries echo around me as the warm ground shakes below my feet, but he doesn't stop. "Do not let go of my hand now."

"But why?" My small, shaking legs scurry after him. "Where are you taking me?"

I stumble as I try to keep up with him. He does not answer me. I glance over my shoulder, searching for my parents' bedchamber, but it's too dark to see anything, the smoke too thick. I'm scared.

"I want Mama," I cry out. "Papa!"

I scratch at Dasinth's hand, trying to break free from his grasp. Dasinth tightens his grip as he drags me into another long corridor—one filled with black flames and even louder screams. I stop smacking his hand then, suddenly very aware of what's happening around me.

The palace, my home, is on fire.

Tears race down my cheeks as I run with Dasinth through the chaos, no longer resisting him. Black flames crackle and hiss around us, licking their way up the walls of the stone corridors. Even the courtyard outside is consumed by the dark flames. I cry as I take in the devastation around me until all of a sudden, Dasinth pulls me behind him and draws out his sword. A shiver runs through me as I sense something coming, something in the wind, as dangerous and dark as the flames around us.

I don't see what happens, but I hear the clashing of swords and Dasinth bellowing. As the ground trembles again, Dasinth picks me up and throws me back down the corridor. I land on my back, my ears ringing, and turn just in time to see the corridor falling down on top of Dasinth. I try to cry out his name, to scream for help, but nothing comes out.

A boy appears in the corridor, and he offers me his hand. "Hurry, come with me!"

His eyes are wide and his hair dark, but I can't move. I can't breathe.

The floor and walls crack, making a huge gap between us, and the boy is swallowed up by the smoke in seconds. More black flames rain down, looking like a burning black star and flooding through the rest of the corridor towards me. Disoriented, I pull myself to my feet, my hearing still muffled, and curl up against the broken wall, the floor nothing but a ledge at my feet.

While the rest of the palace crumbles around me, the black flames continue searing down from the sky, destroying everything in their path. Some of the flames skirt by my feet and burn my toes through my slippers. I scream and pull myself closer to the wall, covering my face with my little hands.

Over the sound of my heart pounding, I hear wings beating like thunder.

I lift my head and look up into an eye of pure gold. There's a giant monster flying in the air right above me, lowering itself. Its black and gold scales smother every inch of it, and its giant wings spread out so far. The smoke completely clears from around me, the flames burning out

4

quickly, as I realise it's a dragon from the legends.

The fierce, massive creature continues to watch me before lifting its head, and I see there is someone riding on its back. A boy much older than me with twilight hair and unfamiliar armour, the same black and gold as the dragon. There is a symbol painted on his chest that I have never seen before, a dragon and a crown wrapped around each other.

The boy looks right at me, taking my breath away with how intense his stare is. There's a long gold scar on his tanned face, and his dark hair is blowing slightly in the breeze. On top of his head rests a magnificent crown.

I know that crown well. It's my father's crown.

My breath leaves me as I watch the boy, and he watches me too with hate burning in his eyes —a hate I feel for him too. Blood drips down his head from the crown onto his cheek, and he wipes it away, his eyes locked on mine. My legs shake as I force myself to straighten. I am the princess of The Drifting Kingdom, and I will not die cowering before anyone.

Tears stream down my cheeks as the boy

watches me, and I want to scream at him. He leans down, whispering something to the dragon, and I know I'm going to burn at his command. The dragon roars at me with nothing but ash, blood, and smoke. I scream, holding my stomach, praying that my death will be quick and easy.

Instead of eating me, instead of my death, the dragon and the boy fly away over my ruined kingdom, my parents' kingdom, and it's burning with the fire of dragons...

A hand grips my shoulder tightly, sharp nails digging into my skin to pull me awake. I blink dazedly at the shadow hovering over me. It takes me a moment to register who the beady eyes belong to. "I asked you a question. You would do well by staying awake in my class to answer it."

Sister Gabriella squeezes my shoulder, her yellowed nails breaking through my dress into skin. I stare up at her, making sure not to wince or give her a reason to punish me. Her punishments are the worst, and I really don't want to spend the rest of the day bleeding.

"Forgive me, Sister," I reply, shaking my head at the memories.

They're just echoes. Echoes of my past. And sometimes my present is far worse than the past. If I don't answer her soon, I will be reminded of that.

"Failure to pay attention again will result in punishment. So, what is your answer, *Princess*?"

I cringe at the use of my title. She only ever refers to me as princess when she really wants to embarrass me in public. I've tried so hard to forget about the life I once had before the king brought me here. It's funny how a single word can take me back to that day.

I clear my throat. "Could you repeat the question so I might answer it, Sister Gabriella?" I try to keep my voice as neutral as possible to not anger her. The convent is run by her, a priestess of the new religion that was forbidden back when my parents ruled. The usurper king indulged in their teachings and gave them the spare castle my parents had used for summer breaks. He also gave them many churches and gold in exchange for keeping me protected.

Protected. The word makes me want to laugh. And gag.

I've endured years of their so-called protection. It's nothing short of torture. However, in the back of my mind, I'm ever aware of how their torture is still better than what comes for me.

"I asked you to explain to our holy class the name of the god we worship tomorrow on Nyx?"

On the day my parents were slaughtered by a boy on the back of a dragon. A boy who became a ruthless king after he stole my father's crown. I blink back any emotion, swallowing down my true reaction like I've trained myself to do, before answering.

"Ciagid, the protector of the dragon race. It is their sacred god."

"Correct." She tightens her grip on my shoulder before moving on. "In a few week's time we shall celebrate Ciagid with fire-works, magic, and feasts across the kingdom. We will celebrate the might of the dragons, and the king who brought them to us. Now, how many dragons will celebrate with us?"

No one answers right away, so she

continues on. "There are two hundred and twelve dragon riders registered at the Citadel, and I expect each of you to name all of them by the end of this class."

"Yes, Sister Gabriella."

I mumble the words along with the others. When there's an unexpected pause in Sister Gabriella's usual spiel, I peer at her from across the room. Her beady eyes lock on me alone as she stands perfectly in line with the centre of the chalkboard, her liver-spotted hands clasping the beads wrapped around her bony waist. She doesn't even bother hiding the sneer that forever taunts her lips when she looks at me.

My blood boils as that old but familiar fear threatens to creep its way over my shoulders. I refuse to let her see it. She thrives off it. I tug my cloak hood over my face and resume picking at the edges of my desk. After so many years trapped in this prison, forced to sit at the same desk and wander the same bland halls, day in, day out, never allowed to leave them, there isn't much left to pick at.

"Can any of you tell me where the dragons originated from?"

Although Sister Gabriella's question is directed to the class, I have no doubt she's still looking at me, waiting for me to crack. I slice my nails deeper into the wood, pretending not to hear her. I know everything there is to know about dragons, just like I know the devastation their riders like to inflict from their backs. I can still smell their fire at night when I go to sleep.

Elliot answers the question. He's one of the few males who were imprisoned here alongside me. Gods above, I can't believe how long ago it was. Only ten years ago? Almost eleven. Sometimes it feels like I was born in this convent.

"The Hallowed Kingdom," Elliot says with an air of smugness. "It was recorded that the first dragon eggs were found inside a mountain by our great king, Erax the Vindicator, and the first ever dragon egg hatched for him." He moves excitedly in his chair, ever the teacher's faithful little pet.

"The king's closest confidants were next to find eggs and bond with their dragons,"

Elliot resumes. "Then each rider flew to our lands once the dragons were of age and a good size, roughly two years after they hatched, although for some dragons, it can take five years until they fully mature."

Although I can't see Sister Gabriella, I know she is smiling at his response. The old crone loves to go over the history of our great Dragon King whenever I'm in the same room as her. She seeks pleasure in reminding me that I'm only trapped here because of him, and that I only breathe now because he spared me that night, he brought us here as prisoners. That's all we are at the end of the day—prisoners of a war started by our parents.

"Very good answer, Elliot." She claps her hands twice, her one form of praise. "You are turning out to be an exemplary acolyte in training. Others would do well to learn from you."

Another slight at me. I ignore it and flick a chip of wood onto the floor.

Elliot glances back at me, that same old sorry look in his eyes. I don't remember much about him from before we were conquered. His father served in my mother's court, and I believe we shared the same governess at one point, but other than that, he was just as strange to me as everyone else when I was brought here.

Sister Gabriella turns her attention to the board behind her. "Now. What colour of fire does the king's dragon breathe, and what makes its flames different?"

I place my elbow on the desk and rest my chin in my hand, my focus straying to the window beside me. Through the thick iron bars, I can just see the beginning of the forest stretching beyond their hold. I've memorised every tree on that stupid border—painted them a hundred times over in my prison cell they call a room. It's the cruellest reminder of all, really. To be able to see your freedom but never reach it. I think that's why Sister Gabriella always makes me sit by the window. She wants me to look out from my cage and know she is the one who holds the key.

"They're black flames, Sister Gabriella," Elliot replies quickly. "Black flames are a gift from the night dragon god, Nytar, and the

12

dragons who serve him will always breathe black fire. Red flames come from the daylight goddess, Hekai. It is said black fire looks like a million stars burning in the night sky, whereas red flames..."

The rest of the lesson goes smoothly as she drones on about the Dragon King and how glorious he is. My parents' kingdom took to his rule quickly, apparently. He was only a boy when he stole their throne. Just shy of sixteen. Yet he took down centuries of my family's rule before imprisoning me here, vowing to the nobles that he would marry me when I turned twenty-one. When a dragon rider army invades, what can anyone do but bow to flames?

In other words, my life has been one endless nightmare since the day he burned my home to the ground and most of the kingdom with it. I hate how everyone calls him a righteous king when he's anything but. He is far from a noble warrior and protector of the realm. To me, King Erax will only ever be the villain in this tale, and he's as rotten to the core as the acts he committed against my family.

By the luck of Hekai, the class finally ends, and I scurry from the room before the priestess can summon me to her. I rush down the ancient corridors, passing the many granite doors that are always locked in this part of the building. Ivy crawls over the old stone walls and around the windows that let some sunlight stream through. The sound of my boots, hidden well under my white dress, hit the stone as I rush straight towards my only reminder of home.

Dasinth grins when he sees me, his smile somehow making his entire face change from terrifying guard to the happy uncle-figure I know and love. He opens up his arms and I run straight into them, pressing my face to his chest and breathing in his familiar scent.

"Uncle, you're back! I heard rumours, but I wasn't sure if they lied or not."

"Nytar blessed my horse, and we rode well," he murmurs, kissing me on top of my head. I'm terribly short compared to him. I pull away first and smile up at him. The light shines in his dark blue eyes when he looks down at me. "How was your morning, my little maeflower?"

I sigh, and the edges of his lips tilt with mirth. "Boring, as always. Tell me all about your... hunting trip." My voice is laced with sarcasm. I can't hide it when I'm around him.

Dasinth told me repeatedly that he was going away for two weeks for a hunting excursion, but we both knew he was not telling me the truth. Food is never scarce here, not with a forest full of bountiful game. Even in winter, there's still an abundance. Not that I should know of any of this since I'm forbidden to hunt. I'm not even allowed into the king's wood without trespassing.

My uncle waves to the path that leads up to the dinner hall. The bitter cold air, laced with snow, somehow finds its way in to freeze me.

"It was... interesting. Plenty of deer."

I roll my eyes at his answer as we get to a table set out with food, including dozens of my favourite honey cakes. Although Dasinth isn't my uncle by blood, he's all I have left. I know him better than anyone. He was stationed here to protect me once he recovered from his injuries after the invasion. I think someone thought it would be a good idea to have someone I knew around me so that I didn't go insane. It might be too late for that, though. I pick up two of the cakes, sliding one into my pocket before my uncle sees. His grin gives me away though.

"Will you ever tell me where you truly went?" I ask, sliding another cake into my pocket.

He glances down at me, a strand of slightly greying blond hair falling into his eyes. "When you are the queen of this land, you can command me to tell you anything you wish to know. Until then..."

He trails off, and a shiver works its way down my spine. Everyone is well aware that I don't want this marriage to go ahead. The king murdered my parents. I don't see how I can forgive him for that, let alone grow to like him.

I'd rather kill him.

"I didn't mean to upset you, Maelena." My uncle's voice pulls my attention back to him as he gives me an apologetic smile. "Forgive me."

"You're forgiven, Uncle." I offer him a

smile, mostly because he didn't say that to upset me or be cruel. It's just a fact. I'm the last remaining descendant of the Dyminien reign and I've been promised to the king of dragons since I was ten years old. There's no escaping it.

This is my fate.

He clears his throat. "The dragons don't usually leave much of the large deer around for us, so it was a treat to find the ones we did." There was a time when I dreamed about dragons being real, like the old stories of dragon riders who fought a great evil centuries ago and won. Those stories, everyone thought they were that—just stories. Part of our past. History. But the dragons had merely been hidden away from us until recently.

Until he found them again.

Now they are an ever-increasing reality. I see them every time I look out the window of the tower, their scales glittering against the sun or pale moonlight as they soar across the sky. They mostly fly around the ruins of my old home, which can be viewed from everywhere.

It's like I've been locked in a tomb, sealed shut for eternity.

When I haven't said a word in far too long, my uncle tries again. His tone is slightly chipper.

"Any afternoon plans, Maeflower?"

"You're asking what I'm doing on my last days of freedom?"

Other than planning my escape.

An awkward silence settles between us. I blow out a breath, noticing him tensing ever so slightly. I can't imagine he wants any of this for me, either, but his hands are as much tied as my own. He's just a pawn to them—a knight set to guard the queen and make sure she doesn't run off the board. That's all my uncle has ever been to them, and it hurts to know that he wants me to play their game.

"Nothing much other than reading, enjoying these cakes, and maybe some painting. Guess I'll head out and get started on that," I say, breaking the silence.

I just manage to hold back what I really want to say. I don't want to risk giving him a heart attack after he almost had one a few years ago, but most of all, I don't want him to intervene. I know my uncle. He will try to stop me from running away.

He smiles like he can almost see what my secret plan is. He whispers low. "Just don't do anything foolish, my dear."

"Like what?" I innocently answer. "I never do anything foolish, Uncle."

"If the nuns managed to catch you..." He keeps his voice near silent. There are always people listening in this place, and more than once, I've been punished for just speaking out about the priestess or the king. "I'm not sure what I could do, but I won't see them torment you anymore."

His expression hardens, and I nod, swallowing the lump in my throat. "I know," I whisper back. "I really do know."

He touches my elbow outside my room, pulling me to a halt. "The Dragon King will not let you go so easily. I don't think I've met a man more intense and protective over what he deems to be his. The old stories spoke of dragons that hoarded gold and were fiercely protective of it. You are gold to this king, Maelena, who is more dragon and beast than he is man." He somehow manages to speak even quieter. "There is still unrest throughout his kingdom—those who call out for the old ways. Your marriage will unify the people to his side that still call for you to be their queen, so be careful. His kingdom and you are tied to a bond that cannot be severed. The bond must be made."

I pull my elbow away from him, noting the hurt in his eyes. "Do you really want to see me married off to the person who slaughtered my parents, burnt down my castle, took the survivors hostage, including you? He is a traitorous, murdering usurper, and I will *never* give him what he wants. He'll have to drag me down the aisle because I will not be going willingly."

He grips my shoulder, and I can barely contain the wince as he touches the fresh bruises left from the priestess earlier. "If you think all he'll do is drag you, Mae—" He stops himself, briefly closes his eyes, and takes a sharp breath before opening them again. "I've prayed to the gods of old every day to release you from this fate. But there is nothing more I can—"

I know how this excuse is finished, and I

cut him off, tired of hearing it. "I've got things to do. Goodbye, Uncle."

I slam my room door behind me, my hands shaking as I clench them, and I rest my head against the heavy wood with a thump. My uncle sighs on the other side but doesn't follow me. I need to be alone right now. My reflection in a full-length mirror stares at me from across the room. I see only a caged bird looking back at me. My rose gold hair falls down to my waist, and it almost highlights the bright purple specks within the lavender haze of my eyes. My eyes remind me of my father, whereas my hair comes from my mother, and it is distinctive of her line. The mirror is the only time I get to see my parents, even if it's just for a moment.

The king is going to be disappointed when he sees me. I'm too thin, perhaps made worse in my white dress I'm forced to wear for my purity, but the cloak is smothered in gold, and it's clipped tightly around my neck like a noose.

The Dragon King's symbols in gold lie along the hem of the cloak, like it's mocking me that I won't ever escape him. Gold stands for the new Dragon King, whereas red had stood for my father's. It's funny that my hair colour is the exact mix of both. Red and gold. I unclip the cloak, throwing it to the side.

"You can come out now."

My only friend in the world steps out from the closet at the side of my small rickety bed. My best friend, Lochlan, playfully grins at me before lying back on my bed with a groan. "Sister Faye insisted on a three-hour walk this morning in the snow, and I had to read old chants to her the entire time. Even praying to Hekai didn't help me, Lena."

Lochlan is the only one who calls me Lena.

Laughing, I jump on the bed next to him and look up at the ceiling, by his side, feeling his warmth. The stone is cracked, dusty, but the bed is comfy at least. Lochlan works for the priestesses as a servant, mostly translating old texts for them.

"At least she didn't make you read to her during her bath this time."

Lochlan lets out a painful noise. "You promised we would take that secret to our graves!"

"Speaking of graves," I say. "How is our escape plan going?"

He leans up on his elbow, looking down at me with his deep brown eyes. "All planned perfectly for tomorrow." I hand him the cake from my pocket, and he happily takes it. He eats as he tells me the last details of the plan. Until now, we both agreed I shouldn't know anything about the details in case the priestesses hurt me to find out the truth. But none of that matters anymore. In one more day, I'll finally be free.

"Tomorrow morning, one of the servant girls, Aki, is covering for you at breakfast. She works predominantly in the gardens and won't be missed. We'll be claiming you aren't well and need to stay in bed."

Hope flickers in my heart, threatening to come alive again. Hope that I might escape my fate at long last. I trust Loch with my life. He was from the castle, like me, but his family were nobles who refused to bow to the new king. They were killed, and Loch was sent here to live in exile with the rest of us. Most of the people here were children orphaned on that day, but Loch is like me, and he doesn't support the king.

I can't help but look at him for maybe a second too long, my heart pounding. His light brown hair looks so soft, shining in the sunlight coming in through my small glazed windows. He wears all black, which is typical of him, and his dark shirt has gold seals running around his cuffs. Some of the buttons are loose, and I have to force myself to look away from them, my throat turning dry.

Sometimes I've found myself fantasising about how things could've been between us if I were a free princess and he were a noble. We might have become best friends then, too. Maybe even more, since royals are allowed to choose whoever they want to be with. At least that was the way for my father and my grandfather and so on.

Although I was the first girl born to the line, I like to think I would have chosen Lochlan, and in another life, he would choose me too.

However, in this life, in this *prison*, it's too risky for him to even talk to me in public, let alone touch me. The punishment would be a slow and painful death if we were ever caught alone together, and I'd never risk that. I have no idea if Lochlan feels that way about me, but he's had my heart from the beginning, and I have a feeling he always will.

Lochlan was the only one brave enough to talk to me when I first arrived here. He used to sneak into my room and tell me stories that made me laugh so hard I cried. He made it possible for me to breathe through the nightmares and always held my hand when I needed someone. Those nightmares still come and go, but I don't wake up screaming anymore. No. The nightmares haunt me in the day now, and I won't ever escape them. I can escape the Dragon King, though.

"There's a cart leaving for the shore," Lochlan says. "They won't notice us in the back with the crates. We've paid them enough to make sure."

I nod, trying hard to control my excitement. "How did you convince your friend to help us?"

He winks at me, and my heart lurches for a moment. I wonder how exactly he convinced the servant to help, before I tell myself to push it to the back of my mind. It won't matter tomorrow. We'll finally be away from here. "We'll get off at shore and then board a cargo ship that's headed east." He pats his chest pocket. "Already got our papers and new certificates ready to go. Nearly cost me a kidney, but there's enough coin left over for us to have a good start."

He shows me the travelling papers and our new identity certificates, and I stare at my new name with tears in my lavender eyes. Violet Gruve. It's so beautiful seeing it in person. I had wanted to pick a name in memory of both my mother and father, but Loch felt it was safer to pick something that had no obvious connection to them or my former life. I pass the documents back to Lochlan.

"Where will we be docking?"

He stretches his arms. "Miseiss, the place where your mother came from. Figured you'd like to see it? You might need to cover up your hair, though. It's too obvious, but then again, we'll be long gone before they even realise." He glances at me a little nervously. "We won't be able to stay in one place for very long, remember? It's too dangerous."

"I know. We'll always be on the run." I blink up at him, nodding. "I'd rather run free than be trapped in a cage."

I rest my head on his chest and listen to his heartbeat; its rapid pace matches the beat of my own. He's as excited and no doubt scared as I am.

Only one more day and we might finally be free!

We've waited so long for this moment. Soon, this will all be over, and we can finally start living our lives again. Tears fill my eyes at the thought of leaving my uncle behind. I'll miss him, more than he might ever know, but I can't endure this anymore. And I refuse to marry the king even if it would unite our people. It's not like they will harm my uncle once they find out I'm gone. With his experience in battle as well as in court, he's too useful to be discarded, or else they would have done so already. Besides, they've never hurt him before. It's only ever me they hurt.

My uncle will miss me too, but he's strong and will get over it. Or maybe he'll come looking for us, and we can be free together. Either way, I *have* to do this. My fate has been sealed in those papers, and come tomorrow, there will be no going back. Only forward.

I hear his familiar heavy footsteps in the hallway outside. His tone is louder than it usually is, firmer even, when he speaks.

"The princess is getting changed. Can it not wait? I do not think you should just go in—"

Lochlan jumps off the bed and into the closet, hurrying through the secret door that leads down to the dungeons towards his room. Mere seconds later, my doors are thrust open and Sister Gabriella storms in with her hands clasped tightly against her pristine white cloak. She isn't alone. Two women I have never seen before hurry after her as I stand just as quickly as Lochlan had jumped. A gold veil completely covers their heads all the way down to the gold ball gowns scarcely hidden beneath them, concealing their faces from me. They are like twins by the way they move in unison, their footsteps barely heard, and are the same height and size. I flick my gaze back to the priestess, who sucks on her thinly pressed lips before speaking.

"It has been decided that you shall meet the king earlier than expected. His people are very eager to see you, Princess, and I'm sure you are just as eager to see them." She snaps her bony fingers at me. "The king has kindly sent his seamstresses here to create a wardrobe for you. You will show them the respect they deserve while they make their corrections, which I am sure there are to be plenty of." She turns her head towards them but keeps her gaze pinned on me. "As I mentioned before, our princess has a rather peculiar palate and often deemed our meals here unsuitable to her tastes." Her beady eyes narrow down at me into wrinkled slits. "Hopefully, she will find His Majesty's food more to her liking."

Every word is like an insult, draped in invisible poison only I'm able to see. The two women ignore her as they walk towards me, and my room quickly fills with rows of hangers holding beautiful gold dresses. I can guess the colour of the choice for tomorrow. Everything is gold. It almost hurts to look at them.

As I'm forced into gown after gown, measured, poked and prodded until I'm flustered and uncomfortable, the priestess watches me with a look of sadistic glee in her eyes.

"Stand straight and lift your head, Princess. We have only a short time to make you befitting and worthy of our king," she says, her lips barely moving around the syllables, "who will arrive in the morning to escort you personally to his royal palace."

My heart pounds with dread as I'm whipped around to face the mirror again. I stare wide-eyed at my shocked reflection gazing back at me, unable to think, move, or even breathe. The Dragon King is arriving in the morning... at the same time as my escape.

CHAPTER TWO

They come for me at night.

They always come for me at night, when the shadows are at their darkest so they can hide their cruelty from their gods. Even though I expect them, my heart thrashes like it's the first time they've come for me, and fear overtakes my body.

I grip my bedsheets tighter underneath me and flick my gaze to the window. The crescent moon hangs low above the forest, its pale light barely reaching the bars on my window. Of course, they would come for me regardless of whether the moon was full.

This is the last night they can do this to me.

They wouldn't miss out on that.

I'm sure this punishment will be for

some insane, made-up reason they will no doubt have gathered witnesses for. Sometimes I think about screaming and running from them—again. Sometimes I think about fighting back like I used to do in the beginning. But if my failed attempts have taught me anything, it's that no amount of running, screaming, or begging for help will stop them.

Not even my uncle can help me, though he never talks about what happens to me on the night of a full moon. I think he's too ashamed to admit he can't protect me like he once did. The former Captain of the King's Guard is just as powerless as the rest of us. Only Lochlan is able to help me, usually the next day, but even he can't stop them.

I close my eyes as soon as they enter, and picture the life we've often talked about— the life that is finally within reach—a home with no bars, a future with no pain, and a place where I can be loved instead of hurting. Lochlan promised to make all that come true, and soon, it will...

It will. It must. Please!

Cold hands grip me by the ankle and pull

me out of the bed. I manage to steady myself before they grab my hair to pull me upright again. The priestess's two favourite acolytes, Sister Breea and Sister Michael, sneer at each other before they each grab one of my shoulders and drag me outside. My bare feet slap the stone ground as I'm dragged off down the familiar, haunting passageways, down the ice-cold stairs, and past the main hall as if I'm being pulled by them through a million sins I never committed. Then they reach the last passageway, the one barely lit with only a single sconce hanging from the wall, and I know we've arrived.

The room they use is always the same one. Dark, cold, empty, with no windows or ventilation. The walls are so thick that my screams are never able to leave them. I swear this room is haunted by a thousand echoes of those screams. I'm thrown into the familiar old wicker chair that stands alone, right in the middle of the room, on a damp stone floor. The sisters tie my arms tightly to the arms of the chair, a precaution they adopted early on in case I try to escape again.

I lift my head, looking up at the tiny bit of

moonlight that claws through the iron hinges of the door. I always focus on it as if that tiny bit of light is my single ray of hope. Years ago, when they first brought me here, I used to pray to their stupid god to save me from them. He never did either. I soon learned that the only one who could save me was myself. And one day, I'd muster the right amount of courage to do it.

As soon as Sister Gabriella enters the room, the last of her acolytes, Sister Faye, seals the door behind her, and then they all turn to face me. Two of them hold lanterns that shed just enough light to let me see the flames flickering and dancing across their hooded frames and their pristinely white robes. I used to think they were ghosts when I was little, sent here to haunt me upon every full moon, until I realised that ghosts were not real and that the figures standing before me were very much real, and they were worse.

The priestess leans down so that her gaze is level with my own, and her murky, almost black eyes bore hatefully into my own. When this first happened, I was ten years old, and I

34

cried for so many nights and days afterward that my eyes remained bloodshot for weeks and I couldn't see properly. She told me it was a punishment from the gods for simply being who I am—or rather, who my blood says I am—and every punishment since has been for that blood in my veins and the title I never asked for.

I stare back at her. After so many of these torture sessions, I no longer speak, scream, or cry out during them. Silence is all I have to hold on to within these four desolate walls. Silence, and a tiny ray of light.

"Tomorrow, you will receive a great honour from our king. One you do not deserve. One you are unworthy to behold, much less receive. There are many in his kingdom who would agree with that statement, but do you know what I think? I think you were unworthy to be born into this world, let alone our next queen."

She grabs my chin roughly, forcing me to look at her in case I dare pull away again. Meanwhile, one of her acolytes rips the back of my nightdress to reveal my back. She loves causing me pain there, and I assume the others don't mind watching. None of them flinch or appear even the slightest bit bothered, not even when blood runs from my back and down my legs to the floor.

The priestess stands and clasps her hands behind her back. "Today, in class, you once more displayed how undeserving you are of the honour that awaits you. In fact, I would almost say you seemed... unhappy about fulfilling your destiny tomorrow. It seems to me that I again must remind you of how happy you should be. How grateful."

What remains of my dress is torn from my back, and I'm completely exposed. I shake from the cold, unable to help it, and I catch the flicker of pure and utter pleasure that gleams in the priestess's gaze. She loves it when I show even the slightest bit of emotion. But when it's fear? She all but drowns in it.

"I am happy," I say, glaring back at her. The lie is repeated so often on my tongue it sounds real this time when it leaves my lips. "I am grateful to accept my destiny, Sister Gabriella."

Keeping my voice as hollow and

emotionless as I possibly can takes work, but I've mastered it. It doesn't matter to her, anyway. She will hurt me either way; this is just a farce for her to pretend she has good reason to punish me in front of these witnesses. She huffs like she doesn't believe me, and internally I wince. It's going to hurt tonight. It's her last chance to break me—or cleanse me—as she calls it.

Sister Gabriella walks around me, her voice low and echoing. "There is a part of me that is happy you are finally leaving us tomorrow. Your very existence is but a stain of the past we all wish to... erase."

Well, tough luck, bitch. You can't kill me. I'm already dead inside.

I bite my tongue. If I can just get through this, I'll be free.

"All those years ago..." Her voice carries to me again. "I was a young acolyte myself when our glorious king first arrived here. He told us that we were worshipping the right gods and that we weren't fools. Not like your parents had us believe." My heart jumps at the mention of them. "Your parents mocked our religion. They claimed dragons were not real, and we were made poor and destitute just from the shame of it. We had nothing. Nothing! Our temple was in mere ruins! But then he appeared, with you near dead in his arms, and as he carried you through the courtyard to us, talking to you, even when you could not hear him, I remember the look he gave you. Even all these years later, I remember the look." Her lips tilt into a sadistic smile. "I had never seen such hatred before. It radiated from him. Do you remember what he said to you?"

I did hear him, and I do remember, but I will never tell her.

His voice still echoes in my nightmares. His words carried with them.

The priestess continues, "This courtyard was in ruins from the war. We didn't live in this part of the castle. It was your parents' summer home. I was merely a slave to them when they decided to grace us with their presence. I wasn't even aware anyone knew about us, about how we still studied the religion in secret. But he knew. We swore to protect you, to bring you up to be a proper princess, one that he will need to unite these lands. There are still fools out there that believe your parents' rule was the rightful one and that he is an imposter." *That's because he is.* "They believe that you are the rightful ruler because you are the last living heir to the royal line of Dyminien."

The cold brush of a whip caresses my exposed back, and I clench my fingers, digging my nails into the wood where there are already grooves from my hands. I hold on, readying for the first whip. It always stings the worst. A cry escapes my lips, even though I beg it not to, as the leather rips through my skin with a sickening noise. The priestess rarely whips me while she talks, her attention usually fixed on one task at hand. But of course she'd go all out this time since it could be her last.

"We were given so much gold, everything within these castle walls, and I will not have you take that away from us!" The whip slashes across my shoulder blades, and I bite my lips to smother my screams. "You *will* be the perfect queen I promised you will be! You will *not* be defiant, sullen, or ungrateful!" Another whip, another piece of leather tearing through my flesh, and blood trickles down my back. "You *will* be obedient and do everything the king asks of you and more, and should I hear that you are even remotely rebellious to our king—should you do *anything* to embarrass me—" She whips three times in a row, and this time my screams leave me, unable to be held back. "Then this will look like child's play compared to what I will do to you, Princess."

Her hot breath blows on my ear, and my skin crawls while tears stream down my face. "Do not forget that the royal palace is full of our priestesses. You will not escape me there. I will always have eyes on you." She claws her nails down the wounds on my back, just for her enjoyment, before breathlessly backing away. I arch my back, sobbing. It takes several moments for her to catch her breath while I tremble in the chair, choking back my sobs. "See to her, then return her to her room. The princess needs her beauty sleep if she is to be ready for tomorrow."

Healing pads are draped over my back, sticking to my torn open skin, and I gag at the smell of them. Chamomile mixed with my own blood. The priestess learned years ago that if she leaves the wounds on my back to scar like she did when I was a child, no amount of healing pads can erase them. She's cruel but not stupid.

They unbind me and lift me off the chair. I sway on my feet, my legs giving in underneath me. The sisters help support me as they drag me back to my room and drop me down onto my stomach. They make sure the pads are secured and working before they leave, locking the door behind them. Silence wraps around me while the embers flicker to their deaths in the fireplace beside me, and I sob into my pillow.

It's over. It's finally over.

I repeat the words until I've no tears left to cry, and exhaustion pulls me into a deep sleep where pain can no longer reach me. I have to believe I'll escape from this place tomorrow, because if I don't and the Dragon King takes me with him, I'm going to jump out of the highest window.

CHAPTER THREE

It's unnervingly quiet as the sun tips slowly over the horizon, its rays flashing beams of red and yellow softly across my sheets. They match the blood that soaked them overnight from my back from the punishment. I climb out of bed carefully and roll my aching shoulders. The healing pads slide off me and fall to the floor.

Gods above, I'm sore, but it's manageable at least. Just.

I dress quickly in the clothes Lochlan hid under my bed for me earlier in the week. His dark leather pants and short black shirt cling to my tender bones. I tuck my hair into his black hat, clipping my locks in place so not even a single strand of rose gold can fall out. It feels a little weird to wear his clothes, but no one will recognise me, and I have to admit it's comforting to have clothes on that are a mark of freedom and not chains.

Lastly, I pull his very worn gold cloak around my shoulders. It smells just like him. Peppermint, like the teas he makes for the priestesses every morning and night. I then grab the daggers my uncle gave me years ago to protect me. He told me to always hide them from the priestesses and use them if anyone tried to kill me and he wasn't around. The irony is that I was never able to use them. I knew, if I did, the priestess would just make my life even more unbearable. Sometimes it was easier to sleep in my cage than fight it.

I pull the daggers out from inside the mattress, a slit I cut and stitched back together so that no one would ever see it. Glancing at the two red blades, my parents' seal still decorates the handle, the gold moon shrouded in a haze of ruby. It is illegal to hold anything with my parents' crest in the kingdom since anything to do with my parents' reign was hunted down and burned. I heard the king offered gold for anyone who brought in traitors or black-market vendors harbouring weapons with their seal.

Tears sting my eyes and I grip the daggers tighter. The king erased *everything* to do with my parents. Everything except for me, and for these daggers, it seems. I always thought it was a little part of my uncle rebelling when he gave me these, some echo of him still saying that he remembers my parents. He is still loyal to them and their rule. I need that hope. I feel like I'm the only one that even remembers them these days.

I sheath the daggers in my cloak, placing them into the hidden pockets with the hilt turned upright. That will make it easy for me to grab them quickly if need be. Loch taught me how to fight with daggers, bows, swords and even an axe. He even claimed I was better than him at times. Blowing out a breath, I look around the room I've lived in for so many years. It's not a room. It's only ever been my prison. Punishments and monthly torture sessions included.

I clench my hands, my body filling with rage. "Good-fucking-bye."

Without looking back, I rush to the

wardrobe and to the secret opening. A girl stands there waiting for me when I push the dresses to the side, leaning on the wall. She's exactly the same height as me, and I've seen her around, mostly tending to the gardens. She's not a priestess in training, but rather one of the servants. The girl Loch told me about. Aki, I think her name was. She nods once at me, her dark blonde hair bouncing.

"May Hekai be with you, Princess. Some of our families still remember who you are, who your parents were, and support you. We pray for you and your rule. Forever the moon queen."

My heart swells and I can only nod in response as I admire her moment of rebellion. These are words that no one has dared utter to me for fear of being killed. To utter them now... it raises a fire within me. People still remember. I place a hand gently on her shoulder and smile at her before I slide through the secret exit. She's risking her life to help get me out of here. I will not forget it.

I hurry down the old stone corridors, my footsteps silent from years of perfecting my hunting skills. The priestesses usually leave me to "reflect" after my punishments, so Aki will have some time to give us a head start. I smile to myself. This could work. This could actually work. I keep running down the dusty, cobweb hallways that always seem like they go on forever.

A breeze guides my way through the darkness, my footsteps echoing through every puddle that eventually leads me to the way out. I turn the corner and step out into the light. Fresh air blows over me, carrying the smell of freshly cut grass from the other side of the tunnel. The tunnel is old and forgotten, smothered in ivy and moss, and full of cobwebs that stick to my arms as I rush to the other side.

The light hurts my eyes as I pause at the end of the tunnel and search around the courtyard, my heart racing. Loch waits for me in the shadows beneath a ruined archway only a few feet away, his dark cloak making him almost invisible. He turns when he spots me and opens his arms, a smile stretching over his lips. I glance around, making sure no one is here, before my feet take off. Running to Lochlan feels like running home. He pulls me into a hug and wraps his arms tightly around my shoulders. For a moment, I just enjoy our embrace, our closeness.

"We're really doing this!" I'm so excited that it's hard to keep my voice quiet.

His soft laugh vibrates down my ear. "I actually thought you were a boy for a moment, then."

I whack his arm, a flush blowing up my cheeks. "This isn't the time for jokes."

I really hope he doesn't think of me as a boy, even in these clothes.

He keeps his arm around my shoulders, careful not to touch my back. He knows what they did to me last night. "You're smiling and not panicking, so the joke worked."

It doesn't work for long. "Where's the cart?"

Loch turns me to the left. "See? It's over there." I follow his gaze and find the cart that he's talking about, full to the brim with wooden crates. Four black horses neigh impatiently as they wait while the driver loads the final crates. "When he's done, we will run and get in between the boxes. They won't see us. We can stay on the cart for the entire journey. This one's going all the way to the shore." He looks down at me, and I smile at him, my heart fluttering. "No one will find us. No one will use you again."

He takes one of my shaking hands, linking our fingers slowly, and I enjoy the warmth of his touch as it tries to calm my racing heart. We wait in silence then and don't dare talk again in case someone hears us. Even though we paid the driver, we can never be too careful. Thankfully, everyone apart from the servants will be in prayer at this time in the morning. They pray to the goddesses as the sun rises until it's quite high up, which is at least half an hour away from now.

The rest of the boxes are finally loaded, and the driver checks his scroll. He scratches his chin before walking to the front and climbing up onto his seat. When he starts whistling but doesn't drive away, we know he's waiting for us.

Loch glances at me and then leans down, bringing his lips so close it's like he's about to kiss me. He could be my first ever kiss. My heart soars and I almost close my eyes. His voice stops me. "Freedom, Princess?"

"Freedom."

I breathe out the single word that means everything to me, and then we run.

I run as fast as my legs will carry me, holding my best friend's hand, our fingers interlocked. We climb onto the cart and duck behind the crates. Loch slides in first, going deeper towards the boxes on the left, and then I crawl to the other side. We smile at each other as the driver kicks off the cart, and the horses begin to move.

The sound of their hooves hitting the ground is like music to my ears. My heart thumps with them, and I close my eyes, resting my head against the crate. Soon the air is filled with that delicious salty breeze I haven't smelled in over ten years. I've missed it. I open my eyes and lift my head just enough to peer over the crates. Out of the corner of my eye, I notice Lochlan watching me with an intense stare, but I'm too mesmerised by the shore growing closer in the distance. The seagulls swooping down on a ship with emerald sails brings tears to my eyes.

I'm free. I'm finally free. I can't believe—

All of a sudden, the horses come to a halt and start neighing in panic. The driver tries to soothe them while something dark, something *huge*, covers us in darkness. Cold, gut-wrenching fear consumes me when nothing but black and red scales spread out across the sky. Fire and roses. That familiar scent. The gold talons, stretching and gleaming in the light.

I've met this dragon before.

Once when I was a child, and then every night since in my nightmares.

The dragon lands on a hill by the shore and sends a gust of wind so powerful it nearly tips the cart. Its roar bursts through my ears, causing them to ring, and I let go of Loch to shield them from the onslaught. Loch looks at me with pure fear in his eyes, and I feel it too. It's over.

We're dead.

Heavy footsteps crunch on the ground outside the cart, and they aren't from the terrified driver.

"Your Majesty!" the driver exclaims. "Can I help—"

"Get back in your seat!" I know that voice too. Sometimes I hear echoes of him in my mind, in my nightmares where dragon fire burns. "You can come out now, Princess. Your little escape is over." I don't respond as I grip the box next to me so hard my nails almost break. *How did he know I was here?* His footsteps pause by the cart. "I don't bite, but my dragon does. Get out."

Tears run down my cheeks—tears filled with the hope for a freedom I was so close to having again. The life I *should've* had. Loch goes to move, but I shake my head and put a finger to my lips. I will face this on my own, and Loch can still be free.

I climb to my feet, glancing at Loch one more time. *I'm sorry*, he mouths to me, but I can't reply. I can't even feel my body as I climb out from the crates and jump down to face the Dragon King himself. My entire world seems to shatter at his feet when I land and look up at him. He's so much taller than I remember. His dragon is huge now, too, standing proudly behind him with its gold eyes on me.

Despite the fear wreaking havoc in my body, I lift my head to look its rider in the eye. His tanned skin has been made rough from his years of combat and dragon riding. But even the scars on his face do nothing to hinder how beautiful he is.

How regal and yet brutal.

He lifts his head and smirks down at me, his thick arms crossed over his powerful chest. As I look up into his scarred face, I hate how he looks as though he was sculpted by the gods themselves. Even the gold scar, running all the way from his left brow to his chin, looks like it was a kiss left by the gods themselves to bless this fucker.

The king is absolutely gorgeous, even if I absolutely fucking hate him. Dark locks of wavy black hair blow in the breeze around his face, and the way the sun hits them makes it look like they have gold strands woven between the tresses. His eyes are perfect emeralds and gold, brighter than any of the jewels I saw as a child in the castle. I remember those eyes the most. They've haunted my every waking moment since that night. Slowly, he drags his eyes up and down my body, and his smirk widens.

"Very fitting attire for a princess. Where were you going?"

I wrap my hands into fists, cutting my palm with how tight I make them. "Anywhere you wouldn't find me, *my king*."

He raises a brow ever so slightly at the way I spit out his title. He will never be my king. He lowers his thick arms, the black scaled leather that covers him from head to toe moving perfectly with his flawlessly toned body as he steps closer. I move back as far as I can, the smell of burning flowers suffocating my senses. He sighs as he rests his massive hands on the two swords clipped to his hips.

At least he's not wearing my father's blood-soaked crown this time.

The edge of his mouth twitches as he looks down at me. Despite the inevitability, despite knowing I shouldn't do it, I turn away from him and run. My hat falls off in the breeze, allowing my long hair to flow behind me. His amused chuckle echoes behind me, far too close. I pull the dagger out just as he catches me, and the moment our bodies collide, I run the blade through his stomach.

At first his eyes widen, as if shocked, but then that smile appears again, and he smirks at me in amusement. I glance down and my own stomach sinks with realisation. The dagger didn't even touch him. It just bent against his armour. The whole dagger bent! What the fuck?

"You're a feisty little thing, aren't you?" He plucks the dagger right out of my hand, regarding the mark on the hilt with a sneer before throwing it to the side. "I almost forgot who you are, Princess, with how fucking beautiful you are. Thank you for the reminder."

I'm shocked into silence at the compliment for a moment. No one has ever called me beautiful. He grabs me in my moment of shock and throws me over his shoulder like I weigh nothing. The other dagger slips out onto the floor, and he stands on the hilt, crushing it. Crushing my hope right along with it. "How many secret forbidden weapons do you have? Do I need to check all of your boy clothes?"

"Let me go, you fucking crown-stealing, murderous bastard!"

I scream, kicking and slamming my fists against his enormous body. His armour just causes me pain, and he knows it. He continues walking as if I'm merely a bug hovering around him, and then he laughs. If the sound belonged to anyone but him, I'd almost admit to liking it. "I prefer you to call me Erax, considering we will be married soon."

Over my dead body!

Erax takes me to the cart, throwing me onto the seat and grabbing the spare reins left on the floor of the cart. I scream and curse him as he easily manages to tie me up to the cart with the straps. No matter how I pull at them, I can't get myself loose. The fucker. Erax looks at the driver at my side, who looks ready to shit himself. "Drive her back and I'll be right above watching. If you want to avoid a painful, fiery death, I suggest you ride fast. The only reason you're not dead already is because her family was well known as manipulative traitors, and so far, it's clear she is just the same."

The driver stumbles. "Thank you, my king."

Erax looks at me once and winks before walking away to his dragon. The drive back is silent, and Loch doesn't dare move from where he is hidden or say a word. The driver doesn't either. Erax lands near the hellhole I just escaped from, and he comes right up to the cart, pulling me off and undoing the reins before throwing me right back over his shoulder. I kick and hit his back, but it's like hitting a wall. A wall that doesn't even flinch or stop.

The priestess and her acolytes come running out of the main entrance just as Erax reaches it. "I am so sorry, Your Majesty, she is —" Sister Gabriella gasps. "You're bleeding! I will fetch the heal—"

"No," he stops her. "I am taking the princess to gather her belongings. Return to your prayers, or whatever the fuck else you do here." As he barges past them, he says pointedly to Sister Gabriella, "If I were you,

I'd pray the gods show mercy for losing my property, Gabriella, because I won't."

I continue kicking and screaming as he walks through them and the crowd of sisters and maids who have gathered to see what is going on. Just before the king carries me through the door, I see the cart disappearing up the hill and through the gates, taking Loch far from me. Taking any chance of my freedom with him.

At least he got out. At least one of us has a future.

The entrance closes behind us, and I keep fighting. I keep kicking and punching him, even though it's like hitting a tree. He's too big, too strong for me to fight off, and that terrifies me more than any punishment the priestesses could make me endure. I knew the king would no longer be a boy but a man. I never expected him to be this huge.

He manages to find my room without any direction and kicks the door open, almost knocking it off the hinges, then throws me onto the bed. I swallow the wince as I land on my back on the clean sheets. The wounds have probably healed by now, but my body is still sore, as if she cut through my bones instead of flesh.

Erax stands in the doorway, blocking my escape. "Get dressed in clothes that don't smell like another male and pack a bag."

I climb off the bed and lift my chin. "I'm not going anywhere with you."

He sighs as he walks towards me, his eyes darkening into slits. I keep stepping back until I press against the dresser. Erax leans down to place his hands on either side of me, caging me in. Now that we're so close, his scent doesn't just brush my senses, it invades them, like a fire set ablaze in a forest. I meet his gaze and hold it with my own fire, one built from pure hate. As if reading my thoughts, he chuckles again.

"Let's clear the air a little, shall we?" He closes what little distance we have between us, his lips so close to my face I can feel his breath on my cheeks. "You hate me, and I hate everything you are too. We'd very much like to kill each other. In fact, I'm willing to bet you're thinking about trying it again right now, aren't you?" I don't say anything, and he smirks. "Believe me when I say I want nothing more than to wrap my hands around that pretty little neck of yours and put an end to your line once and for all. But as king, I have a responsibility to the people of my kingdom, and I won't see you get in the way of that. This could be easy if you—"

"What? Obey you like a good little princess bride?" My sarcastic laugh cuts him off. "You fucking slaughtered my parents! You wore my father's crown, covered in his blood, as you burnt down his kingdom, my home, and then you locked me in here with these monsters until I was old enough to be your wife. All that dragon fire must've burned your brains if you think I'll make *any* of this easy for you. I'll spend every day for the rest of my life trying to get away from you!"

He clicks his tongue, but his jaw tenses. "Royal marriages have been arranged in far worse conditions in our history. I don't give a fuck about you or what you want, but you will be my wife. So, get dressed and pack your fucking things."

I lift my chin despite its tremor. "Or what?"

He picks up a strand of my hair. "I don't like to be pushed, Princess Maelena. You're mine." He drops my hair. "As for escaping me, that will not happen. You don't know this about me yet, but when you try to disappear like mist, I will find you. I always find anything that is mine." He steps back. "I suggest you put on warmer clothes. We're going to be riding on my dragon, and it gets cold."

I glare up at him. I know in reality I don't have much of a choice but to go with him. He'll drag me to his dragon either way. I try to push the thought of riding on a dragon to the back of my mind. It would have been a dream of mine as a child who used to devour any book I could find about the dragons of old. Now it will be a nightmare come to life.

"I doubt the frilly princess gowns you sent me will be warm enough." I cross my arms, casting a glance at the open wardrobe. "Most of them are practically see through."

He follows my gaze to the many dresses hanging from the rail. My pulse spikes as I wonder if he knows my escape route is right behind those dresses. "I didn't send those."

He turns back to me, a frown creasing his forehead for a moment. "I will wait outside. But don't push my kindness, Mist. My patience already wears thin."

"That isn't my name!" I shout at his back as he walks away from me and to the doors. He shuts them behind him, leaving me in complete silence. I look at the wardrobe, knowing I can try to run again, but it would be pointless. They would never let me go. Angrily, I wipe my tears away. A single thought fills my mind... I don't have to live through this. I could end it all as soon as there's a high enough window. Death is no stranger to me, and if this is the life I'm to lead, then I welcome it. But something screams at me not to kill myself, a voice that sounds so much like Lochlan.

Don't do it, Lena. Don't let him win.

But I also can't let him have me either, even if that means joining my parents in the afterlife. The eternal plains where all the fallen stars go to rest.

I look through the dresses, searching for the rags I've been wearing all these years. Someone must have cleared it out when they changed my bed. I scoff at that. They're trying to hide how they treated me, but Erax already knows if his threat is anything to go by. That was the first time I've ever seen Sister Gabriella afraid. I paint it in my memory, a wry grin sliding over my lips. Maybe I should stay alive long enough just to see her get what she deserves.

With none of my old clothes to choose from, I put on one of the long, very sheer, gold dresses and then wrap a gold cloak around my shoulders. I'm not getting dressed in warm clothes like he suggested. Finally, I braid my hair and step out in the long, stupid gold dress that was left for me. Erax looks me up and down, frowning at all the frills and lace of the dress.

"Really, Mist?"

I narrow my eyes. "That is not my name, Dragon King!"

"Erax," he reminds me, pulling his gaze away. "Or your darling, handsome king, if you're incapable of those two syllables."

Fuck. You.

My uncle steps forward from the side of the passageway, his face unusually pale. He doesn't pay the king any attention as he tries to approach me.

"Princess Maelena—"

Erax holds out an arm to stop him. "Even if you are her uncle, she is not to be addressed as that. Anyone who speaks to her will use the title Her Majesty or Her Grace. As for her real name, it is reserved for me now."

I glare at him, my rage for him boiling to an even deeper level. "You can't—"

"I'm the king," he says, turning to me with a smirk. "I can do whatever I want."

I step right up into his face. "One day, I will find a way to stab you and make sure you bleed forever."

He glares back, and I shiver when his words roll over me.

"Keep making sweet promises like that, Mist, and I just might let you." He walks off like he expects me to follow, and when I don't, he waves me to him as though I'm his fucking dog. I look pleadingly at my uncle. He only nods his head after him, suggesting I get a move on with it, and a piece of me dies inside.

How is it possible to love someone so much and yet hate them for not helping you?

Without looking back at my uncle, I follow in the king's wake. We soon enter the front courtyard, where his massive dragon awaits. The beast is just as impressive and terrifying as I remember as a child, only bigger. So much bigger.

"This is Cyrsí*," Erax says, looking up at the beast. "The last of her line."

Like me, I think bitterly, as I follow him over. *Thanks to you.*

Cyrsí looks down and stares at me for several moments with her huge, unblinking gold eyes. I can't help but get the impression she is deciding if she wants to eat me or not. To my relief, she looks away, and I let out a long breath I wasn't aware I was holding in. She lowers herself down for Erax, and her saddle is the same colour as his eyes. Green. Except it's decorated with his royal crest—a crest I've seen before all over the convent. Two dragons devouring each other, one of them breathing fire and the other roses. The

---

* Seer-sye

irony never fails to make my stomach churn. Erax is the fire and I'm the roses, burnt to nothing. That's how it will always be between us.

As we near the saddle, he moves to my side and places a hand on my shoulder. "You'll need help to get on."

"Don't you touch me," I growl, yanking my arm from him. "I don't need your help."

"Because you've mounted dragons before?" he scoffs, crossing his arms. He steps back from me, though. "Go ahead, then. I think I'm going to enjoy watching this."

That smirk that seems to permanently grace his face returns again, and I clench my jaw, refusing to give in to him. This is my chance to show him I'm not that weak little girl he met all those years ago. I'm a woman with revenge in her heart and blood on her lips. I decide to climb the side of the dragon by using her scales as steps. It's surely the only logical way to mount a dragon.

Unfortunately, the dress doesn't help make things any easier, and I hate that the king might be right as I slip—repeatedly. But I don't give up. I keep on climbing, feeling her heart beating beneath her scales. They're as firm as steel and yet so warm beneath my palm. I always thought dragon scales would feel as cold as ice.

After many attempts, I finally reach the top of her and carefully lower myself down onto her saddle. Erax effortlessly climbs up in a fraction of the time it took me. However, he says nothing as he slides behind me and grabs the reins, pulling them tight. My heart races as I hold on to the front of the saddle, our bodies pressed too close together. Dangerously close.

"*Nivaross*." Erax's deep voice caresses the back of my neck.

I turn to meet his eyes, which are already fixed on me. "What does that mean?"

He leans into my space until we're a breath away. "It means fly."

Then the dragon takes off, jumping into the clear blue sky, and all I can do is scream.

CHAPTER FOUR

As a child I often wondered what it would be like to ride a dragon of my own. A dragon who would be my defender and make sure no one would ever see me as a small little girl ever again.

I would drift off during one of the royal tutors' mind-numbing classes, and I'd fantasise about being far away from them, on the back of a dragon, with nothing but the wind in my hair and sunlight on my skin. I never thought I'd get to experience that with the arms of the king of The Hallowed Kingdom and The Drifting Kingdom wrapped around me. Even with the wind whistling through my ears, I still hear his strong heartbeat thundering against my back.

It's all I can focus on.

It's several hours later when Erax calls

out another command, and the dragon lowers herself through the clouds. The sun is still high in the sky when we make our descent. Despite my uneasiness, I cast a glance below. Its gold towers are so tall they can be seen for miles, splintering high into the sky with black onyx dragons curled on top of each one, their heads raised as if looking over the city below. Lush dark green forests and bright yellow fields surround the castle, only to stop at a massive stone wall that encircles the castle lands, with only one gate. A cavern to the right stretches for some distance, and as my eyes drift to it, I feel something strange in my gut. A prison, but a fancy one. The Hallowed Kingdom is spread in every direction, brick towns and pretty cities flooding into the mountains, which make a half-moon shape around the edges of the kingdom, tipped with snow.

There were once six kingdoms, where each one worshipped an elder dragon—Ciagid's gift to humanity. While Ciagid's children, Hekai and Nytar, gave us the night and morning sky, their father gave us dragons—divine beings sent to offer their knowledge and guidance. But man being man, the kingdoms used them as weapons to conquer their fellow neighbours until only two kingdoms remained: my great-grandfather's and Erax's. We'd always known The Hallowed Kingdom would launch another attack, but I don't think my father believed it would happen in his lifetime. I guess he's paid the price for that now.

I fight back my tears and clutch the saddle tighter, focusing on our descent. The Hallowed Kingdom spreads out until the ants scuttling between buildings turn into humans, and heads turn as CyrsíCyrsí swoops overhead, her massive shadow swallowing them whole, but they cheer for her.

They cheer for him too. CyrsíCyrsí swoops above the wall and over the yellow straw fields towards the castle, which is all green stone for the most part, only the towers are made of gold this close. It's an imposing building with windows lined in an asymmetric pattern around the seven levels. At the front is a massive stone door and a courtyard big enough to land a dragon on. The courtyard is filled with five willow trees, the beautiful green branches blowing in the wind. Green roses and their vines have grown all up the left side of the castle, just touching the gold towers, and it strikes me that this isn't what I thought the castle would look like at all.

Cyrsí lands outside the palace gates. The dragonmeyer is already waiting for her, her green colour robes billowing behind her. I've never seen a dragonmeyer before. My father had no need for them since we had no dragons to take care of and they hated dragons. Dragonmeyers still lived in our kingdom with their families, finding other occupations, but they were not treated with honour, not the dragonmeyer's job anyway—to train and look after the dragons. Something about their blood makes the dragons not eat them —or that's what I've read.

The dragonmeyer crosses an arm over her chest as a mark of respect for her king's return. Then I realise she's not welcoming her king home, but rather the beast she tends to. Cyrsí lowers herself to the ground in front of her, the earth shaking beneath her as she lands, and turns to the dragonmeyer. The hooded woman is chanting something to her, but I'm not able to hear what it is. It sounds like more dragon tongue.

Fortunately, there's a staircase beside the dragon this time and a platform leading up to it. I let go of the saddle and prepare to slide off onto it. However, Erax pulls me closer to his chest, and in the blink of an eye, he's sliding down the dragon's body, taking me with him. I have no choice but to hold on to Erax as my voice leaves me in a silent scream. His hand presses against the small of my back, and I can feel the heat from his palm radiating through my clothes.

As soon as we land, I pull away from him. The edge of his mouth twitches as though toying with a smirk. I glare at him and dust my hands down my body, ridding myself of his scent. It clings to me like a flame to dying embers.

Erax approaches one of the many servants gathered outside the palace doors. They line the steps, waiting patiently for their king's instruction. Some of them look genuinely happy to see his return. My stomach twists.

After I stand for several minutes in silence, Erax gestures for me to follow. "Come. Let me show you your home."

Each of the servants bows to me as I walk by, following in their king's wake. I can only stare at them, confused why they look so... happy. None of my parents' servants ever looked quite like this. They were grateful for their employment, absolutely, but I don't think I ever saw them smile and even blush and giggle as they bowed and curtsied. I certainly never saw anyone do that at the convent. Even the sisters were all miserable, apart from Sister Gabriella. I think she enjoyed their misery too much.

Everyone smiles and bows to their beloved king like he is a god walking among them and not a fucking monster. I barely see where I'm walking, as it becomes hard to breathe. I can't live like this. I can't be his wife... I can't...

Erax opens a wooden door, which has two handles and a dragon drawn into the oak across the door itself. The handles are gold, and they might as well be chains wrapped around my neck. "You're not my prisoner.

You're my wife. If I wanted to keep you here, I'd shackle you to that bed and make sure you never leave it." He kicks the door open and flicks his chin towards it. "You're free to come and go as you please. Just watch out for the traps my grandfather laid around here. Some of them can be quite nasty, and I don't want that pretty face of yours getting hurt."

I lift my chin, refusing to show the effect his words have on me. He called me his wife. Not his betrothed or his intended or even his future wife. His wife. And I hate the way my heart jumps when he does it.

"So, I'm safe to wander the palace halls?" I ask. "No one will try to hurt me?"

Something darkens in his gaze as he narrows his eyes into slits. "If anyone tries to hurt what belongs to me, it will be the last thing they ever do before my dragon eats them and burns their home to ashes." He takes in the blush threatening to creep over my cheeks, and his scowl deepens. "Don't get it twisted, Mist. All you are to me is an object, a piece of my property, and an attack to the king's property is an attack to the king himself. It's my duty to protect what belongs to me, and you belong to me—whether you accept it or not. So, yes, you are free to walk my halls. Take a fucking stroll through the gardens for all I care. Just don't get yourself blown up, because then I'll be really pissed, and you don't want to see that. Got it?"

I can only nod in silence, unable to reply to him verbally. His disdain for me has never been so clear. I really am just an object to Erax. I might become his wife on paper, but in reality, I'll only ever be an object. An object he doesn't even want to belong to him. As I look up into his eyes, it's clear to me that the king hates me as much as I hate him. This will never work.

I never wanted it to.

"I'll send for you when I'm ready," he growls, pulling away from me. "In the meantime, you will make use of the bathing room next door. You smell like a fucking stable."

I pull my lips back in a snarl, glaring at him as he approaches the door. "My sincerest apologies, Your Majesty. Sister Gabriella must've forgotten to hose me down before you arrived. I'll be sure to pass on your feedback to her in due course."

He pauses for a moment, as if contemplating what I said, his hand clenching the door handle. He opens the door and I storm inside, waiting to see if he will dare to come into what must be my room. Blood pounds in my ears as I watch him, my rage increasing. I'm well aware of my smell. I just spent several hours on the back of a dragon, but more than that... I still have blood on my back from last night.

Erax closes the door behind him instead of coming in. I hear no key twisting in the lock, and I wonder if he was telling the truth about not treating me like a prisoner. But even then, it's just empty words at this point. A prisoner without chains is still a prisoner when there's no way out of the cage. I know because I've lived in one for years now. This one is simply prettier.

I cross the room into a bathing chamber where the sound of trickling water carries to my ears. It comes from a small bamboo fountain tucked beneath an impossibly high, sun-shaped window—one too high to reach, never mind jump from. It's been so long since I've seen a bath like this. There are no puddles turning to ice on the dirty floor, no grime on the walls or the bathtub itself. The water is clean and fragrant, and the towels folded on a rack beside it are as white as clouds. I walk over and touch them cautiously, my fingers straying to the matching robe and slippers on a wooden shelf next to them. They feel like clouds too.

And they smell amazing—clean and fresh.

I set the slippers down and focus on the enormous vanity mounted onto the wall across from me. Countless products, soaps, essential oils, and perfumes decorate the shelves. I recognise some of the luxury brands from when I used to sneak into my mother's bathing chamber. One of those bars of soap alone is worth more than everything I own.

Is this a trap? I step farther into the room, locating the water closet. *Does he think I'll fall for this?* I can't help but feel like he's teasing me and that any second he'll burst out from the shadows laughing and have me taken to the dungeons.

Still, as I take in more of the gorgeous

chamber, finally locating the huge tub, I desperately want to enjoy this, even if it's just for a moment. I lock the door and strip down to nothing, shoving every garment in the clothing basket by the vanity. I then lower myself slowly into the bath, hissing through the brief pain as the water hits my back. In spite of this, the warm water is an instant relief to my tired, aching body, and whatever remains healing on my back is thankful for the reprieve, too.

I slide down, sighing as I rest my head against the tub, my chin skimming the water. For the first time in hours, I let myself think about Lochlan and our failed escape plan. It only failed because the king arrived early. Had he not, I'd be on a ship right now, headed to my mother's homeland. Instead, I'm trapped in his home, albeit in a very nice, and much needed, bath.

At any rate, there's no going back. I've got to focus on a plan going forward, and to do that, I need to familiarise myself with my new cage. That's the first step to finding a way out of it, and luckily for me, I've already done some of it.

It was years ago, but I remember poring over old maps of the Dragon Palace, and blueprint proposals that had been approved by the former king himself. My grandparents paid a large sum to have the documents smuggled over the border to them, but my father didn't seem that interested in them. I found the documents stuffed away in his study, pressed under an ancient tome that barely clung to its bindings. I made sure to memorise every inch of them, more curious about the dragon aspect than anything at the time. I had no idea how useful my curiosity would turn out to be. It might just be what saves me from this place.

From what I'd discovered at the time, the Hallowed Dragon Palace is mostly like every other palace except for two major elements. The first is the fact it is a fortress, designed to be impregnable. The second is the dungeons, where they keep their prisoners and, more importantly, their dragons. The floorplan itself covered three large parchments and spanned for several miles beneath the city grounds. The tunnels used to transport live-stock to the dragons from all across the city.

If I'm to get out of here, those tunnels are my best bet. I need to find them to make sure they're still accessible.

I pull myself from the bath, reluctant to leave its warm embrace. I have no idea when I'll next get to bathe like this. But freedom is more important than comfort. Comfort can easily be given, whereas freedom can only be won. Or taken back from those who took it away from you in the first place. Either way, freedom isn't something so easily obtained most of the time.

Sometimes, you've got to fight for it.

And that's all I can do now, really...

Fight.

I dry slowly, savouring the way the towel practically caresses my body, then I place them in the wash basket before turning to face the vanity. This could be my last chance to experience something like this for a very long time. My reflection takes me by surprise, as it always does, but I try hard not to focus on it. I'm going to enjoy this moment of pampering. Goddess knows I deserve it.

I pull out several of the products and

gently massage them into my skin despite feeling that it's almost silly to be using them. It's not like they'll erase the decade-long bags under my eyes or the trauma buried deep within my bones. But they smell nice, and it's been so long since I've been able to smell nice like this.

I'm still worthy of things that make me feel pretty inside.

I spray my body with a small bottle of lavender mist and then twist my hair into a loose braid down my back. My eyes stray back to my reflection and tears well in my eyes, briefly distorting my vision.

I'm still worthy, period.

I step back into the bedroom and really look at it for a moment. It's a room fit for a queen and reminds me somewhat of my mother's private bedroom. Soft furnishings, floral wallpaper and thick fur rugs on the wood floor. At the other side stands another door that leads to a massive walk-in clothing chamber. It's almost the same size and length as the main room. I open the wardrobe, surprised to find a variety of items and not a single gold dress in sight.

What surprises me the most is the leggings. I take a pair of them out, running my fingers over the soft black material. Fur lines the inside of them, yet they're completely weightless in my hand. My parents would never let me wear something like this. Princesses were only ever allowed to walk around in pretty dresses and ball gowns. My mother would often reprimand me when I trudged into the castle with mud on my skirts from playing in the gardens. I always hated wearing those stupid dresses. Now I'd give anything to hold one of them again and smell her scent. To even just hear her shouting at me to act more like a princess and not a stable hand.

A matching tunic hangs beside the leggings. I pull both items on and secure the tunic with a rose gold belt found in one of the many accessories hanging inside another wardrobe. Each section of the clothing chamber is divided by occasion—gowns for formal events, outdoor garments for hunting and riding, and everyday wear, which is where I found the leggings and tunic. A final wardrobe stands alone by the window, its doors gilded in intricate details. It's empty when I open it, but the gold railings and level of detail on the outside tell me that it must be important. Royal attire, maybe.

Pity I won't find out. I don't plan on sticking around for that long.

I slide on a pair of brown boots and fasten the laces from my foot all the way to my lower thigh. They're just as light as the leggings and tunic, and equally comfortable. The fashion here is so different from when my parents had ruled. Their taste was more about how many jewels you could hold on your body and buttons made of diamonds or jewels. So many buttons. I remember feeling like a bag of coins at formal events, my clothes jingling when I walked.

The thing I hated most was the small but sharply cut gems the servants would weave painfully into my hair. It had all felt uncomfortable and unnecessary to me, but to my parents, it was all about tradition. And they really cared about upholding traditions, especially the royal ones.

My steps are soundless as I walk to the door. I can do this. I am not a weak princess, born to be captured and bred for what children I can have with him. I want to be free, and I have to give myself every chance.

Or I die.

If not the death of my body, my soul will die if I'm forced to be his wife. My hand shakes as I turn the handle, and the door just opens to an empty corridor. Sounds echo from the south of a vast corridor, filled with steel knight statues and framed paintings that look old—and priceless. But nothing alive is in the corridor. I can barely believe I'm getting a moment of good luck before I run straight to the servant stairs I spot at the end of the corridor and slip inside. The room has three doors and a hatch on the floor, just like I suspected it might do. The blueprints I saw said there were escape hatches into the tunnels in every servant quarter because they wanted their servants to have a chance to escape if war came. My father laughed when he was told about this and claimed it was a weakness to want the weak to escape.

He was wrong for that. I'm now the weak he once laughed at needing an escape, and I just know he would be happy I am getting a chance at all. He'd tell me to run. The hatch is heavy, my hands slipping several times as I lug it open until it slams on the floor, and I brush my hands on my tunic. Heat blows into my face when I look down and see nothing but a staircase leading into something hot and glowing red at the bottom.

I don't give myself a second to talk myself out of this mad plan before I climb down the warm wooden stairs and drop down onto a rough stone pathway—through a lava pit. Lava pours in rivers on either side of the path and spits embers occasionally. I trust in the gods, in the bit of luck they have already given me, before I start walking fast down the pathway. The path empties out into a stone-tiled dome, and there are four tunnel entrances to choose from.

Crap, which one?

I rub my arms as I take them in, listening for any clue of which way I should go or even just a little sunlight, but there is nothing but darkness in each one. Left. I'm going to take the far left one. I don't know why I choose it, but every second I pause is a second closer to the king finding I'm missing and figuring out where I am. I take one step into the tunnel, only for a metal gate to suddenly begin to slam down behind me. Thick hands wrap around my waist, yanking me out of the tunnel just as the gate slams down in front of me and lava floods the tunnel, brushing against the gate where I was just standing.

Breathless, I turn and come face to face with a furious Erax. "Do you want to burn to death, Mist?" He moves so close our lips are inches away. His eyes flicker over my face, down to my lips, just for a second. Something twists in the depths of his eyes. Lava pours closer to us, but neither one of us moves out of its way. "This place is full of traps designed to kill you. None of these tunnels lead out, you utter fool."

"I'd rather be a brave fool trying to escape you than your stupid and quiet wife!" I snarl right back at him.

I step away, but he grips my wrist, tugging me against his body. My heart races as he runs his hand through my hair and shakes his head. "I don't want you to be silent and stupid, Mist. Just my queen, like our kingdoms need. I don't want you either, but I will not let you go."

Liar. "You won't get me."

He smirks and lets me go, walking away from me. "We will see. Stop trying to disappear like mist. I'll see you anywhere."

CHAPTER FIVE

ERAX

There are still ash marks on my hands, sourly reminding me of the stupidity of my new bride. I turn the corner of the corridor and towards the royal quarters, past my room... Why would she try to escape again so soon? And why, in the name of Ciagid, would she go down there where there was nothing but certain death awaiting her? I told her about the traps, but she clearly doesn't trust me.

Can't really blame her for that, though.

I did kill her parents and burn her kingdom to the ground.

Is this going to be our entire marriage? My life spent saving her nice ass from her own petty, foolish mistakes? Why does she have to be so fucking beautiful? She nearly took my breath away when she climbed out between those carts and I saw her for the first time since she was a child. I could practically hear her heart racing, and her eyes were so wide with shock, bright with fear, but strikingly beautiful. Too fucking beautiful.

And then her lips... Fuck, her lips are the perfect shape for devouring.

Didn't expect that.

I hate to admit that I've dreamt of what she'd be like and detested my dreams when I woke. I should hate her for her very existence, for the blood swimming in her veins, for the mistakes her parents made, and the fact that she clearly still loves them like a loyal daughter so blind to reality. I'd almost pity her if I didn't hate her guts so much. Her blood will always come between us, whether she's beautiful or not. Hopefully, she doesn't get herself fucking killed though before she's of any use to my kingdom. Then we're really fucked.

I rub my face, trying to get her out of my

head, but I see her long rose gold hair that looks soft and yet strong enough to wrap my hand around to arch her pretty neck. I can't stop seeing the swell of her breasts, the inviting dips of her hips. She smelt like divinity, and I wanted to sink into her, to taste her, to know what it would be like.

Mine.

My dragon's feelings on the matter swarm my thoughts. She's possessive of her, and those possessive thoughts are spreading straight through me in all the worst ways. Fuck, my dragon sees her akin to gold, a treasure, and she won't let me risk her treasure. Dragons do not share.

Those possessive feelings make me feel like I'm going fucking insane. My boots slam on the stone as I cut through the castle, ignoring anyone who calls for me. I push open the doors to the private courtroom, letting them swing shut behind me, and the bright sunlight shines across my eyes from the open archways. I'm greeted with a boisterous, sarcastic laugh.

Noble leans on the massive solid red oak table that occupies the middle of the room. "I heard she stabbed you, Goldeye. Now how did that tiny, pretty little princess of yours manage to stab the king?"

Something about him, my best friend, calling her pretty, clenches my stomach. I have to admit, I was fucking impressed she had the balls to stab me, even if it was futile. Burning jealousy crawls up my throat at the mention of her, and I gulp, pushing down the urge to fry my friend to a crisp over a mere compliment. *Mine.* My dragon barely speaks to me in my mind, and her words usually aren't understandable, but I heard her loud and clear.

Mine. She's mine. Ours!

Noble is still waiting for an answer when I push my dragon's emotions out of my head and slam my thoughts down into a pit of ash. The room fills with my courtiers, all waiting for a similar answer, but most of them wouldn't dare say a word to me. They are just people who care about nothing more than themselves, and the price I pay for being king is working with them in the name of peace. Doesn't mean I have to like them. I barely even trust them.

"She's quicker than she looks," I say. "It won't happen again."

Noble laughs louder, his blond hair glowing in the light, and I resist the urge to punch him and ruin his pretty uniform. "Why are you covered in ash? You look like you've had a fight with a fireplace, and regrettably lost. Who was worse, the princess or the fireplace?"

Fuck's sake, I don't even want to tell the smug bastard. He would laugh his head off if I told him what she just did in a stupid attempt to flee.

A softer, silky voice interrupts. "I could help you get changed, my blessed king." A small, soft hand runs down my arm. I blow out a frustrated breath and face Ambre. I'm sure she'll be happy that the princess is here, even if no one else is. They're not related by blood, which is lucky for her, but they're family as far as her dad, Mist's uncle, is concerned. *Mist.* I should not have given her a nickname like that. She is no friend of mine. I'm seriously losing my damned mind.

Ambre is the same age as the princess, and maybe it would be good for the princess to have her as a friend. Ambre tucks her long blonde hair behind her ear, blinking her eyes once. Annoyingly, she's wearing barely anything. A slip of a red dress covers roughly half of her body, and it's near enough to see through. I can definitely see her nipples through it as she saunters closer. I don't know her well, but her father brings her to the castle on occasion when he attends court. Why she is in here is a mystery to me.

Usually, I'd be interested if a woman as beautiful as she was flirting with me, but right now, all I can think about is the hot-headed princess I've just dragged out of one of the traps that my grandfather set up for intruders.

Loyalty is a choice, and I am going to be married. Now she is here, I won't touch anyone else. Not that it will be difficult to keep to that mental promise. My cock seems hard in her presence alone, as if she's controlling it.

Ambre hands me a glass of wine and I take it, downing it quickly before going to the table. "No, and you shouldn't be here. It's for my council. Leave."

I don't bother looking to see if she goes. She's wise enough to obey my commands.

I place my hands on the table, looking over the clay map of my kingdom. The entire kingdom is spread out on one table, like it's small and not the home to millions whose lives rest on my shoulders. Red markers are littered across my cities like a fucking infection.

"There are more rebellions?"

Noble and the priest look between each other, but it's Noble who dares answer me first. The first of my closest riders are out flying, or I'm sure one of those fuckers would explain it quicker. "The rebellion is growing in alarming numbers." He pauses. "Perhaps the marriage will—"

The unrest, now named the rebellion, brews fast throughout my large kingdom but mostly in the old Drifting Kingdom lands. I banished that name when I claimed the lands and made it all The Hallowed Kingdom lands, but the borders that don't exist anymore are marked with the rebellions of the traitors that keep appearing. It has always been brewing, like a storm that I can't

G. BAILEY & SCARLETT SNOW

quite escape, but now it's here and it's fucking suffocating.

I cut him off as he goes on and on about the politics of marriage. "I don't want to talk about the princess or the marriage."

Priest Jean clears his throat. "Well, I did not leave my prayers for no reason. This meeting was called to speak about marriage, my king."

Noble frowns at me. He is my closest friend, the second one to take a dragon in my command, and my brother like the other riders. There's no one in this world I trust more than him. I know him as much as he knows me, and he probably is wondering why exactly I'm so flustered. Noble points at the red markers. "There's unrest in the cities."

I cross my arms. "I'm well aware of that."

"Yes, but it is worse here." Noble points to the map. One of the third largest cities, which was free of rebellion only last week. "They blew up several of the military establishments, including family homes. I hate to inform you that many children were injured, some of them killed. The rebels are getting riskier and no longer give a fuck who they kill to make their point."

Priest Jean sighs. "They poisoned some of the lakes around here with dragon poison, imported in. The dragons frequently drink from several of these lakes, but they were smart enough not to and sensed the danger." Anger floods my senses. To hurt a dragon is an insult to the gods who protect us... and if they killed one, I wouldn't show them any mercy. "The gods tell me that this marriage will calm the rebellion and bring much needed peace. The sooner you are married and she is with child, the better."

No pressure then. I want to snap at him, ask him if he has met the princess. She won't give me a day's peace if she has her own way. "I am also aware of this, but I still don't want to marry her. She's the child of my enemy— people I've spent my whole life making sure ended up dead for their treason. Do you remember what they did? Do you recall how my people's bodies littered the streets that day we walked through them?"

Silence rings between us all, as we all know it's true and there isn't a single thing I can do about the past. I'm a king, with all the power in the kingdoms, except over her. I made sure her father brutally died for everything that he had done in these kingdoms. Marrying his daughter is the ultimate fuck you, but it was never in my plan until I saw her eyes. I think back to the first moment I met her. She was pressed against a wall of the falling castle, smothered in smoke, and yet so rebellious in the face of my dragon. My dragon was a creature she had never seen, who promised a certain death in the name of fire, and she didn't blink. I was covered in her father's blood, for fuck's sake, and she still faced me down, like a warrior, and I couldn't kill her.

I couldn't kill her, like I should have done, and that decision has always haunted me.

I knew keeping her alive would mean only one thing; she would become my bride, or she'd die at my hand. I ended up choosing the former, and I don't fucking know why.

Noble touches the map. "People are still loyal to her family—to her name. The wealthy at least are. The poor are completely behind you. We need unity and it would be a war if you didn't marry her. The rich still remember the times when her parents ruled and how they benefited."

No one dares speak about how exactly they benefitted. The mines. I clench my jaw at the memories I will never be able to erase from my mind. Those mines were truly one of the more horrific sides of the kingdom I witnessed when I took over. Her parents were obsessed with diamonds and gold, with being richer than any other kingdom, like a race that only they cared for. Even if it cost hundreds of thousands of their people's lives and forced half a million of them to live underground and suffer to serve them.

Any crime that was committed, whether it was as simple as robbing a slice of bread because they were starving, or murdering someone that was trying to kill them, they were thrown into the mines. Sometimes they were sent down there for no good reason. Their families were sent too, whether they caused the crime or not. They were always taken in the name of the royal family, and once in the mines, they were as good as dead.

They were locked in, never allowed to see daylight or feel fresh air again. Children were born in the mud and died in the same cave, never once seeing an ounce of the outside world. I don't think they even got to see the sky or what a cloud looked like. All the death, pain and misery, just to mine for gold and diamonds to line the pockets of a kingdom that did not care for them. They didn't even need the coin; the king and queen were more than rich enough.

The mines were the worst of it, but slavery was rife in their kingdom. And it was brutal. Freedom was a dream, not a reality, until I flew in on my dragons and burnt that kingdom into a free flame. "The nobles will never be happy because I took away all their slaves, burnt down the mines that fed them gold and diamonds, and told them to fucking serve me or die. I will fly my dragon around that city and burn the fucking cowards to stop this madness," I snarl. I've absolutely had enough of them, the ungrateful little shits. It's been years. Years of this crap.

"Maybe we can make a new plan that doesn't involve burning a city down and naming you a tyrant," Priest Jean softly suggests, ever the voice of reason. It's not surprising. He looks old enough to be a god in his white robes and wrinkled skin. "We'll bring the marriage forward. There's no point holding her here and not making the marriage immediately happen. The kingdom can celebrate the marriage and wait for news of an heir. It will be exactly what we need."

Yes, a celebration for them, and a fucking life sentence for me.

"Go and get the preparations ready. You are dismissed." The rest of my council leave, and I lift my head, looking out of the arch windows, over my kingdom hidden behind the mountains. I was hoping my bride would be some obedient, quiet princess that wouldn't push me too far. Instead, she is defiant, fucking gorgeous, and is already driving me to the point of insanity—and we've only been together a day. What will an entire marriage do to us?

"You look like you're about to marry an ugly troll instead of a princess." Noble pats my back. "Smile, you fucker. She sounds amazing."

"I hate her and everything she is," I grumble. "This marriage is going to be nothing but a transaction between us."

"Look, she's been locked up in that boring shithole, and she knows you're the person who killed her parents. So she ran and tried to kill you, so what? It makes her smart and capable." He looks over the kingdom with me. "Traits you might want in your future queen who will be the mother of your children one day. She's probably not even aware of how evil her parents were, as she was just a child herself when you killed them. I know that you want to hate her because of who she was born to be, but give her a chance. Like you said, she's gorgeous, strong-willed, and you usually like that in women. Your dragon likes her, and she hates everyone. I see all this as a good sign. Give her a few orgasms and your usual charming smiles, and she will soon love you like the rest of the kingdom."

I push off the table, heading to the door. "It can never be more than a contract for our thrones and people. She hates me and I hate her, and I don't plan on changing that. End of story."

Noble laughs like it's the funniest thing he's heard all day. "I've never seen you this riled up, my brother, and you've never lied to me before."

I'm tempted to growl at him, but I leave it, knowing I'll just prove his point. My guards begin to follow me as I storm down the corridor, and I stop mid step. I want to be alone. "I'm going for a ride. Make sure there are guards stationed by the princess's room and she doesn't end up dead while I'm gone." I pause, adding as an afterthought, "Watch her, but unless she is in danger, don't let her see you."

They bow, leaving me to it, and I trust them to follow my orders. I don't need their protection, but she clearly does. My dragon is waiting in the courtyard, so in tune with my emotions that she knows that I need to fly before I explode in flames. When I'm up in the sky, I don't feel like I'm chained to the princess, or to the kingdom below, unable to escape either of them.

CHAPTER SIX

I wake up to something I haven't smelled in years.

Pancakes.

The scent teases my senses the moment I open my eyes the next morning. My mouth instantly waters, as if recalling what they used to taste like, a mere flicker of my childhood before it was taken from me.

I reach for the breakfast tray on my nightstand and carefully place it beside me on the bed. The pancakes are fluffy like clouds and drenched in maple syrup. My eyes all but water as I rush to cut a bite, and I nearly moan at the sweet taste on my tongue. I haven't been allowed anything sweet like pancakes and maple syrup in years. Sister Gabriella used to say it would make me fat, and she controlled every little bit of food I ate.

A sharp pang stabs me in the chest when I take another bite, instinctively recalling the mornings spent eating stacks of pancakes with my parents on my birthday. When I close my eyes, I can still see them sitting at the table, even smell the freshly clotted cream on my mother's lip, or the honey mixed in my father's tea. It was one of the rare times we ate together, and my birthday pancakes quickly became one of my fondest memories. It was so rare to eat with them, and I cherished every moment we got to spend as a family.

I eat the rest of the pancakes slowly, acutely aware of how vastly my taste buds have been deprived of sweet things. It's like eating them for the first time. The pang in my chest is soon replaced with guilt as my thoughts stray from the past to the present, and to Lochlan in particular.

Lochlan...

Wherever he is, I hope he manages to find delicious food like this. He deserves it more than me. My appetite shifts at the thought of him, and I struggle to finish the rest of my breakfast, but I force every bite down. I need my strength now more than ever. I devour the rest of the pancakes, the plump strawberries next, and finally the sugar-coated mandarin until the plate is empty. I take a sip of the orange juice, the ripeness dancing on my tongue. I can't remember the last time I drank fruit juice like this; the convent always watered ours down.

Once I've eaten, I lie back on the bed, my belly full and thirst quenched. It's then something else rises within me from last night. Something I never expected to feel in the presence of my enemy... something I felt with Loch. Lust. Desire. A burning that hovers in my blood, begging to be quenched. With Loch, the feeling felt soft and quiet, but with the king, it is violent and destructive.

The king's face, bathed in golden flames, sears its way through my mind. I shut my eyes but his lips and that smug smile of his still taunts me. It doesn't make sense. I have hated Erax for more than half my life. I've spent years nurturing my hatred for him and carving it into the very depths of my being. How could he make me feel... that?

He almost kissed me last night, and for the shortest of breaths, I had wanted him to. I wanted to know what my enemy tasted like, what those murderous lips would feel like pressed against my own. Would they taste like blood, like the blood that forever coats his hands? Or would they taste like something else entirely?

Last night was the first time in my existence I wanted to find out.

I need to get out of here as soon as I can.

A knock on the door jolts me from my thoughts. Thank the gods. I straighten on the bed and dust the pancake crumbs from my nightdress, relieved to find the king's face vanishing from my mind. At this rate, any distraction is welcome.

"Come in."

The door opens and two servants enter. I recognize them immediately as the king's royal seamstresses, the same ones who forced me to wear dress after gold dress at the convent while Sister Gabriella watched.

Whatever they're here for can't be good. It's not like I need anymore garments now.

I search the area behind them, relieved to find only another servant following them. The guard places a highly decorated trunk in the centre of the room. The seamstresses pause at either side and bow.

"Your Grace," they both say, then the shorter one gestures to the trunk. "King Erax has sent you generous gifts to be worn during the wedding ceremony."

It's the first time either of them have spoken to me, and I'm surprised to find no... malice in their tone. More surprising is the fact they referred to me as their grace.

My stomach clenches and I dig my nails into the mattress. "Gifts?"

"Yes, Your Grace. It is customary for the king's bride to wear a royal wedding jewel. Every new queen of The Hallowed Kingdom is made a new piece of jewellery to wear on her wedding day, and it will be added to the collection. There are currently many pieces for you to choose from. The king has requested that you personally be allowed to choose."

Together they lift the trunk, revealing various pieces of breathtaking jewellery. The sunlight filtering through the room bounces off the rich necklaces and bracelets, causing them to glitter like stars. Velvet boxes line the far side of the trunk, and at first glance, I assume them to be rings. It's not until I walk over and cast my gaze over the strange objects do I realise they are earrings. Not the kind I'm familiar with, but the kind that follows the shape of your ear.

I reach out for one of the boxes, pausing to glance at the seamstresses, as though this is some kind of a trap. The smaller one nods, and they watch me tentatively pick up the earring. My heart hammers in my chest as I run my finger over diamonds so sharp they nearly cut me. There's so many of them. This trunk alone could rebuild a city. My parents' city.

My city.

I swallow down my spite, holding back the resentment, and focus on the task at hand. After perusing the objects, I settle on a delicate necklace with a short gold chain and a small dragon-shaped pendant that hangs from its centre. The jewel carved into its eye glimmers a pale silver-blue in the light, reminding me of the moon. The seamstress nods and reaches into the trunk, drawing out one of the many unopened boxes.

"Might I suggest the dragonquartz bracelet and ear wrap to match, Your Grace?" She opens the box and holds it beside the corresponding bracelet, almost identical to the necklace except the dragon pendant is wrapped around the jewel like it's cuddling the moon. "Or perhaps Your Grace would prefer our newest arrival, the sunlight rose quartz, to complement her beautiful hair?"

I shake my head, drawn to the dragonquartz. It reminds me of home, like the moon always does, but more than that, it reminds me of strength.

And I really need as much strength as I can get right now.

The earring, or ear wrap as the seamstress called it, is just as beautiful as its counterparts. It's shaped like a dragon, with moon quartz for the eye, but the wings are stretched out this time, and when the seamstress tests its fit on my ear, the gold tips poke out between strands of my hair. It's beautiful, all three of the items are, but I don't say it. I will accept nothing willingly from their king. How I'll manage to successfully keep that up, and for how long, I don't know, but I've got to at least try. He is my enemy after all. The fact he is to be my husband will never change that.

The seamstresses close the trunk, and with a click of the smaller one's fingers, the guard returns to carry the trunk outside. The women follow him, and I frown at their backs. Surely that isn't all? The ceremony is coming far too quickly.

"Is that all?" They turn to look at me, their expressions as confused as I feel on the inside. "What I mean is, the dress... Will I have a say in that?"

They do not answer, and my gut twists uncomfortably. Silence never means anything good. At least not in my experience. Silence has often resulted in something worse than a response. Something I could never mentally or physically prepare for.

This room, this palace, this kingdom— it's suffocating.

And it's not like the king forbade me from wandering his palace. He did say I could take "strolls" so long as I don't get myself blown up. The king doesn't need to know that I'm going to use those strolls to take in every inch of my prison so I can fetch a way out of it.

After another long bath, I dress and make my way through various parts of the castle. When I stumble onto a library, I spend hours searching the shelves for anything that might help me. The variety of books is impressive, and I only stop reading when I smell something savoury. It's then I notice someone has brought dinner to me, leaving it on a table by the library window. It's evening already?

I eat the delicious meal, my nose still buried in a book. Once my stomach is full, I head back to my room for a short rest. I sit on the bed and focus on my breathing, but as I look around the beautiful chamber, I keep seeing it as another cage. The walls feel like they're closing in on me. I feel sick sitting here in silence. There's nothing to distract myself with or stop my thoughts from racing. I need to get out of here again.

I grab my robe and slide it over my shoulders. Opening the door, I peer outside for the guards I sometimes find lingering there. None stand guard tonight. There's something immediately suspicious about that, but my anxiety is too high to let me ponder it. If I don't get out of this room right this second, I'll scream.

Wrapping my robe tighter around me, I head in the opposite direction to where I went earlier. The air is distinctly different the moment I step foot into the vacant hallway. It's colder here and the smell of burning ash does not fill my senses. The walls are also lit with more sconces that allow me to see the intricate patterns carved into the stone beneath my pink slippers.

I pause at the end of the corridor, my gaze falling upon a strange glowing insect perched on the edge of a flowering locus. The insect is small enough to be missed if its wings didn't glow a bright, bioluminescent shade of blue. Its light alone is strong enough to beam against the stone wall, highlighting more of its kind gathered within the crooks. There's an almost tangible pattern about the way they've positioned themselves. I follow the pattern, curious to where its spirals might lead and extra mindful of my steps this time. The last thing I want to do is accidentally trigger another trap again.

I follow the trail cautiously. I've never seen insects like this before. They remind me of dragonflies, almost exactly like them, except their eyes and wings glow like sapphire stars. So strong is their light that they eventually replace the sconces to guide my way, leading me down a long spiral staircase to an old wooden door covered in vines with the same bioluminescent glow. Thick layers of dust cover the wood, and the handle has all but crumbled on the floor, leaving only a gaping hole behind. The door doesn't look like it's been touched in years.

I peer through the hole, seeing only more of the glowing bugs on the other side. Surely something so beautiful couldn't be a trap. That is probably what the trap maker would want their victim to think, yet I'm inexplicably drawn to this door. I hesitate. I can't risk getting myself blown up again, and I really don't want to wander too far and end up crossing paths with a guard.

Or worse, the king himself.

I turn around and make for the stairs again. As curious as I am to find out what's on the other side, I'm not brave enough to take the risk.

That's when I hear it. The distant lulling of waves crashing over rocks.

My entire body freezes to the spot as childhood memories come flooding back to me: summers spent lounging on the beach with sand in my hair and the whole west ocean stretching before me. It was rare that my governess would take me to the beach where my parents had private access. My mother was always frightened I would somehow end up drowning in the water, so she never let me go, but my governess—my dear, sweet governess, who was killed in the fire—would take me there as a treat when I pleased her with my studies.

As if called back by the waves themselves, I face the door again. It's been so long since I've heard their beautiful whooshing or felt the coldness of their salt water caress lapping at my feet.

Excitement builds within me. In the time since I turned around, the bugs have gathered in the keyhole, leaving just enough room to insert a key. One of them flies down to perch itself on what remains of the handle.

I bend over, grasping the crumbling object in my hand and turning it over in my palm. To my utter surprise, a slightly rusted key rests half-lodged inside its mechanism. A tinge of cautionary fear begins to cloud my excitement. If I believed in signs, then this is as good a sign as any. It's like the gods themselves want me to open this door.

Despite the king's caution echoing in the back of my mind, I pick up the key and insert it into the gap. The bugs use the tip of their wings like claws to hold on to it and slowly turn it around. The door opens out into a corridor, only it's not really a corridor. It's more like a passageway typically found in a cave.

The bugs cover the walls on either side of me, glowing in that same spiral pattern as before. But it's not them I'm focused on now.

It's the exit at the end of the passageway where the sound of waves can be heard. The ocean has always calmed me—always made me feel less alone in a world burning around me.

Relief washes over me when I step out of the exit. There is a beautiful rocky lake shore stretched out far in front of me, hidden under the branches of thick trees so it cannot be seen from above. The branches are so tightly woven that it is hard to even make out the moonlight through them, but it's bright enough here.

What strikes me as odd are the torches outside the exit. There are two of them at each side, mounted on iron dragon statues with their claws holding them in place. Both of them are lit. I scan the shoreline again. The only other inhabitants are the dragonflies skimming the surface of the lake and embankments like flickering blue stars.

There doesn't appear to be anyone else out here. I stretch up onto my toes and yank out one of the torches. Lochlan would tell me to turn back. I can just hear his voice in my head. For as long as I've known him, Loch has a fear of deep water and the things that could lurk in their depths. I've always been the opposite. The lakes and ocean have only ever smelled like home to me, and this is the closest I've been to home since it was taken. I've waited years to do this.

I'm not going to turn back now.

I now believe there is a reason I have been brought here tonight. None of this is coincidence. The gods don't believe in coincidence, only fate. And so do I.

Extending the torch to help guide my way, I approach the water's edge. Pebbles replace the grass beneath my feet and crunch against my slippers. I slide the torch between two rocks to hold it in place. My hands shake with excitement as I remove my robe and slippers, placing them a foot away from the torch.

There's enough light now that I can clearly see where I'm going. I roll my nightdress to my thighs and tie the edges into a knot just below my hip. Goose bumps rise over my body, and the cool night air feels amazing against my skin, like an embrace from an old friend.

I dip my feet into the water, surprised to find the temperature warm. The beach at my parents' had been cold but invigorating. The water here is so different. As I step further into the lake, it's like sliding into a warm bath. I close my eyes and allow myself to just soak everything in. The way the current laps at my body, the softness of the kelp cradling my feet like down pillows. Gods, even the salt in the air fills me with a sense of relief I haven't felt in such a long time. It's like I'm dreaming again instead of succumbing to nightmares.

It's like I'm home again.

Something brushing against my leg prompts me to open my eyes. I glance down at the murky depths, figuring it's some kind of fish swimming by. With only the moon and stars to light my way this far out, there's little I can see under the surface. The fog creeping in from the opposite side is only making it harder. Where did that fog come from?

Disturbed water rippling beside me makes my heart jump.

I turn around, scanning the water around

me. I catch only a glimpse of something flicking out of the water in the corner of my eye, something huge and glistening. It causes the current to change and for the waves to pull me in deeper.

I dig my heels into the slick floor and lift my head to prevent any water from entering my mouth. The salt stings my eyes as the waves crash over me regardless, dragging me to its depths. The water is no longer a warm embrace but an icy chokehold where rocks claw at my body and algae ensnares me in its slippery trap, causing me to sink faster.

I keep trying despite the weight of the water crashing down on me. In my heart, I know I've come too far to give up now. I've endured too much just to surrender to this water when I know there's still a small chance I could be free of all this. I use it to fuel my determination, and I manage to push myself high enough to gasp a single breath into my lungs before I'm dragged down again.

The breath is enough to keep me going.

I swim against the current, giving everything I've got until there's no energy left in my bones. It's then that I see it—the blast of electric blue light hurling its way towards me. It lights up the bottom of the lake, illuminating the depths to which I've been brought. There are eyes down there.

Dragon eyes.

The water muffles my screams as I try to swim away. With only moments to spare, I use the last of my strength to grab hold of the kelp, but I'm too weak.

Too exhausted to pull myself up.

I close my eyes and brace myself for the impact—and whatever will follow it. But nothing comes. There's no pain, no burst of light slamming against my body.

Only darkness.

Then air rushing through my body to fill my lungs again.

I roll to the side, my chest burning as I cough up water, and dig my fingers into a rock-hard surface as cold as ice. For several moments, I can see and do nothing other than that, my vision completely blurred and my eyes stinging.

Something pulls me back, away from the lake, and settles me by the torch in the rocks.

A blurry silhouette moves through the light towards me and leans down.

"Lest you become that frost dragon's supper, you might want to be more careful next time."

His voice cuts through the coldness around me. I blink up at the stranger, finally able to see again. He straightens on his feet until the full moon eclipses him and offers me his hand. I take it cautiously, allowing him to help me up. He is blond, tall and pretty in leathers that are the same scaled ones that Erax wears. Another rider. Even in the moonlight, he looks distinctly familiar as if I've seen him before, yet I can't quite place him.

"What... happened?"

"You tell me. It's not often frost dragons come so close to the surface. That one down there has never been ridden and usually eats anyone in this lake as a snack. Many have tried and failed to tame him."

He moves to the side, and I cast my gaze over the entire lake. I almost can't believe what I'm seeing. Everything around me is completely frozen. The lake and embankments, even the footpath leading from the palace to the lake itself is now covered in ice. *How* did this happen? The stranger looks at me curiously while our quick breathing clouds the air with smoke, entangling with each other.

"I thought frost dragons were extinct," I say. "What is one doing in that lake?"

"They were *nearing* extinction," he counters, "but King Erax managed to save them. They never come this close to the edge, though, and I've never seen one with..." He trails off, as if suddenly realising who he is talking to. He pulls off his cloak and drapes it over my shoulders. I'm too cold to shrug it off. "Dragons are especially territorial during breeding season. You're lucky I got here when I did, or you'd be burnt to a crisp right now."

Burnt to a crisp. I shudder at the thought.

"The name's Noble, by the way. Ironic, I know, given I just saved your ass."

I pull away from him and tighten his huge cloak around my body, sneaking a closer look at him as I slide my cold feet into my slippers. Even in the moonlight, I can't see anything that makes me trust him. He looks more like a member of the king's royal court, and he must be if he is a rider. A loud huff blows across me from my right, and I spin, looking into the forest to see dragon eyes reflecting the light. I can see red eyes and brown scales but not much else. "Don't mind my dragon; he is curious about you because you smell like Cyrsí Cyrsíand you're not her rider."

I turn back to Noble. It's so secluded out here that I can't think of a good reason why he would be at the lake late at night. Unless... the king sent him to look for me? That seems plausible, given his clothes. Maybe he is a close member of his court.

"Thanks for saving my ass," I say, "but I'd like to know what really brought you here. Did *he* send for me?" I keep my tone neutral but add a little emphasis on the word *he*.

Noble picks up several rocks from the ground and throws one of them across the lake. It skates to the far side and lands on a frozen lily pad, shattering the reeds there to pieces like broken glass. "I mostly came here for the same reason as you—to get the fuck out of that palace and breathe some fresh air. I've been coming here to swim since I was a kid." He throws another rock. It doesn't land as far, and he curses under his breath. "Anyways, doubt I'll be doing that for a while until it thaws and the dragon goes back to its nest as he usually doesn't bother riders. He came higher than usual." He glances down at his hands, and the ice on the lake reflects in his dark eyes, causing them to gleam. "Don't suppose you know how to unthaw the lake you've frozen, do you?"

"I didn't freeze it."

He laughs. "Well, the dragon certainly didn't, or you'd be dead. No one survives their ice fire. It's more brutal than even Cyrsí's legendary black fire."

I bite my lip, unsure if I should tell him the truth. Maybe I did miraculously freeze the lake somehow. Maybe it was a miracle. I don't know. But what I do know is that I'm out here, alone, with a complete stranger who, although he saved my life, is also huge and carrying a sword at his hip with his dragon watching me. I'm vulnerable. I need to appear less so even if it's a lie.

"I'm still getting used to my power," I say. I wonder if the dragon could have caused it. I have heard about dragon riders possessing rare abilities due to the unique link they share with their dragon, but I'm not bonded to a dragon.

No. It doesn't make sense for that to be the reason. Something else must have caused this, and I need to figure out what.

"All right. I don't mind sharing this place," Noble says, pulling my attention back to me, "so long as you don't grow to be a pain in my ass?"

The way he says that reminds me of Lochlan and the way we would tease each other. In fact, in this light, he almost looks a bit like him. A sense of longing tugs at my insides. Gods, I miss Lochlan so much. I miss having someone to talk to. I miss having a friend.

"Cat got your tongue, snow pixie?"

I shake my head absently. "No, I'm just... trying to figure you out."

"Oh yeah?"

"I'm a stranger to you. Better yet, a prisoner. Your *king's* prisoner. Why are you being nice to me?"

He laughs, the sound sharp and without any mirth. "I'm a lot of things. Nice isn't one of them." He shrugs, tossing another rock. "I just can't help but feel sorry for you."

My blood seethes at the remark. I don't need his pity. But I do need an ally if I'm to get out of here, so I hold back my spite.

"I feel sorry for you too," I say, affording him a faint smile. "I froze your lake."

His lips tilt upward at the sides, hinting at a genuine smile. He follows my gaze back to the pond. I'm no longer looking at its shiny surface. I'm looking at the wall surrounding the palace. A wall I will never be able to climb.

"I know that look." There's evident scorn in his voice when he speaks, and I glance at him from the corner of my eye. "There's no way you're getting over that wall unless you can carve wings from that ice of yours. Flying is the only way in and out of this palace without the king's say, and unless you can bond with a dragon, you're stuck here."

His eyes linger a moment too long on the

wall, long enough to tell me he has tried to escape from here once. Perhaps he failed, just like me.

Something pulls his attention behind me, to the passageway. I glance over my shoulder. The second torch remains lit by the entrance, and the doorway is unoccupied. However, Noble's frown deepens. He throws aside the remaining rocks and wipes his hand down his dark clothes.

"Now, are you coming back with me, or are you going to be a pain in the ass after all?"

I'm not ready to go back. I don't think I'll ever be when I know what waits for me. It's just another prison. But I'm not as anxious as I was earlier. This encounter has somehow managed to help calm me down, and that's really what I needed. I can't run away from my fate forever. Not for some time, at least.

Grabbing my robe, I follow Noble back to the passageway. He picks up the torch and leads the way, the halo of light guiding our path down. In the days I've been trapped here, I have seen a number of guards come and go outside my room. Noble has never been one of them. He looks too young to rank above them, yet his clothes say otherwise. They are of high quality, and the cloak he draped over me is as thick as the king's had been. Except, their scents couldn't be more different to each other. Erax had smelled like fire and roses, whereas Noble is like freshly fallen snow settled over treetops at dawn. Odd considering the other guards' scents had carried that faintest hint of burning leaves. There is almost something familiar about Noble's scent.

"Is Noble your real name?" I ask.

"Fuck no. You think I'd let my mother call me that? I would have crawled back inside her."

His reply almost makes me laugh, and I blush. I bite my lip and continue to follow him. "Then why *do* they call you Noble?"

At the end of the passage, he opens the door and waits for me to step through. In the firelight, I notice his forehead is creased with a frown. I step over the threshold back into the warmth of the palace. Noble follows me a moment later.

"It's a long story," he says, leading the

way again. "One for a night when you're not busy preparing for a wedding and we both have wine."

My stomach lurches at the reminder. My wedding.

"Where are we going now?" I ask, my breathing quickening as I follow Noble up the stairs to the training wing that is usually full of soldiers learning the ranks. It's empty now.

"My orders were to bring you back." He lowers his voice, a playful gleam in his eye, and glances back at me. "Don't worry, Ice Princess. The pond remains our little secret for now."

For now? I nod despite my growing unease, still not entirely sure that I can trust this man. I guess only time will tell if I can. In the meantime, I need to gain as many allies as I possibly can while I'm trapped here. Noble could be a good start.

He takes me back to my room. Four guards stand by the entrance, and the door is slightly ajar. There's usually only one guard stationed outside. My heart drops to the pit of my stomach. What if there's another tradition I haven't heard of that takes place the night before the wedding? What if, in this kingdom, your bonding occurs prior to etching your vows of eternity into the stone of fate?

What if it's all completely different here?

My heartbeat increases with every step towards my room. The guards immediately move aside for Noble, confirming he is of higher rank to them. I can't even turn my head to look at him when we stop outside. My gaze is rooted on the door, my focus latched on the familiar scent permeating through the gaps.

Noble pushes the door fully open. Erax is leaning against my dresser, his hands clenching the sides, with his gaze fixed on me. I can barely hear my thoughts over the racing of my heart.

"Remove the cloak," Erax growls. "My wife does not need it."

His eyes stay narrowed on me as Noble removes the cloak, exposing my slightly damp body to the cool night air filtering through the balcony window. He closes the door behind him, and all the blood drains from my body as I try not to squirm under the king's gaze. Now we are alone, and I've nowhere left to run.

"Where were you?" he asks after several moments of tense silence.

I lift my chin again, hoping to convey a sense of calmness I do not feel inside. "I went for a stroll, in the gardens, like you said I could."

The irony is that I went for a stroll and nearly died, again, like he told me not to. I don't tell him that.

He scoffs and crosses his arms. "Funny. I sent several guards to the gardens, yet none of them could find you."

"That's because I—"

"I might have given you free rein of the palace," he cuts in tersely, "but as of tomorrow, you are to be my wife. I expect to be able to find my wife whenever I have need of her."

I clasp my hands behind my back, more to prevent myself from clenching them. "And what need did you have of me this night, Your Majesty?"

His upper lip twitches. With what emotion, I am not sure, but it makes my heart stutter and skip a beat, nevertheless. He crosses the room towards me. I consider stepping back, but my feet remain glued to the floor, as frozen as the pond had been.

"I think you know what I need, Mist." His fingers slide under my chin and lift my head, forcing me to look up at him. "I need you to wash that other male's scent off your body."

My voice catches in my throat. "I—I already washed today. There's no need to waste—uughh!"

He sweeps me over his shoulder before I can finish speaking. I grab hold of him to keep myself from falling, painfully aware of his hands on my upper thigh, now sliding over my behind. My body immediately flushes at the contact.

Without a word, Erax carries me into the bathing chamber where a bath has already been drawn. He drops me into it. I let out a surprised scream as the water surrounds me. The water is lukewarm, telling me it's been waiting a while, but it's still amazing against my cold, shivering body.

Despite my distress, I'm instantly warmed by its embrace, and my clothes no longer stick to me like sheets of ice when I surface again. I gasp for air, both relieved and shocked by the ordeal, and grasp the sides of the tub. Erax holds me down to prevent me from standing, his eyes blazing with fury. I've never seen such rage burn in a pair of eyes before. It's almost... feral-like. Like staring into the soul of a dragon and not a man at all.

"Erax... leave," I demand.

He pauses, watching me too closely. He tilts his head to the side, a growl that is terrifying slipping from his lips. "Mine."

I freeze in the water, feeling almost as cold as I was in the lake, as he backs away to the door. He looks over his shoulder at me. "No male touches you again, Mist. Next time, they die."

CHAPTER SEVEN

There's a man screaming for help in the corridor outside my room. Sitting up in my big girl bed, I clutch my doll as my eyes dart to my bedroom door. I shouldn't go out there. I should stay in my bed, like a good princess. The bells above the castle begin to ring, and I know them well. There is an intruder in the castle. The man screams in pain again, and my body shivers. I've never heard someone scream like that before. Although his shouts are too far away for me to understand what he is saying, my feet itch to move.

Stay in bed, Mae. Mother and Father wouldn't like it if I got out of my bed at night.

For once my thoughts do not stop me from crawling out of my bed. I wince as my feet touch the cold stone ground and grab the lantern from my nightstand. Its glow lights my way as I walk *over to the door and pull it open. I expect to see the back of my guard, but there is no one outside. Flames flicker from the oil lamps hanging on the walls stretching at either side before me. They grow brighter towards the end of the corridor where a man screams on the floor. My guard stands over him with his enormous sword slammed right through his stomach. I shudder and feel a little sick at the sight of so much blood. There is so much of it that it pools around the man like a puddle, glistening under the firelight like the sun against black water. I instinctively step back, my heart racing so fast I can hear it in my ears. It doesn't block out the man's cries though, or his pleas for mercy. My guard growls at him.*

"Th-the princess... I only wanted to ta-k-ke her so they would listen to me! I wouldn't—have —hurt her!"

"You are a traitor to your kingdom," my guard snarls at him, and then he slams his heavy boot against the man's head. The man screams even louder. He is so thin that I can see all his bones poking through his rags. Who is this man? Why did he want to take me? As a princess, I've always known there are people out there who

want to hurt me, so it doesn't make sense why this man says he wouldn't. A cough escapes his mouth, blood spraying across the stone as he chokes out a reply.

"Her parents are evil—monsters—but they might... have listened... if I got their princess." He starts to cry as more blood pools out from him. "They took my whole family! They threw them into the mines like they were animals for my brother-in-law's crime. They even took my baby girl. She was only two weeks old!" He coughs again, louder and wetter than the one before, as his breathing begins to slow. "I thought if I... took the princess... they would let me trade... and maybe let me... see her... my little Marissa..."

He goes still as death greets him, and I'm frozen to the spot. He's dead. He's dead. I repeat the words over in my head, completely shocked and unable to move. My guard kicks the man's body to the side and pulls out the sword impaling him. Everything rushes back to me then as the bells suddenly go silent. I shut my room door and run back to my bed, burying my face into my pillow. My cries are smothered but no less painful as the name Marissa etches itself into my mind like a scar carving through my flesh.

The man had just wanted to see his baby.
His little Marissa.

My chest heaves when I wake, breathless and sweaty, and stare up at the unfamiliar ceilings. The quilts around me are too heavy, smelling like strange flowers, and they are suffocating me as I push them off and crawl back to the headboard, hugging my legs close to my chest. What was that dream? Was it real? I don't remember, if it was. Mines? What was the man even talking about? I'm sure he was just another assassin sent to kill me as a child. He wasn't the first, and had I still lived in that castle, he wouldn't have been the last.

I focus on my breathing and try to slow it down as I stare around the room. I feel as trapped in this room as I did in that nightmare. I'm not sure what has kept me going until now. With free rein of this palace, it would have been easy to join my parents and at long last be at peace with them. I could have drowned myself in that lake had I wanted to. I had enough time before Noble came and the whole thing with the frost dragon happened. There are plenty of stairways I could have thrown myself down, and I've lost count of the number of windows that don't have bars on them that I could have jumped from. I simply... haven't, but now I really wish I had. Tomorrow, my life as I know it will be over. I might never get the chance to see Loch again. I'll be married to the very king who has haunted my nightmares since I was a child.

My hands clutch the sheets and I close my eyes. The ritual and marriage will begin tomorrow morning, if it isn't morning already. I should appreciate this bed because I doubt I'll even be in this bed at all tomorrow night. I'll be in his bed, where he'll force me to do whatever he wants to get an heir. It's not like he wants to do this either. The king hates me as much as I hate him, and lust will always pale in the shadow of hatred.

I lurch out of the bed and run to the door, grabbing the cold metal handle. It clicks open and my legs are running before my mind has caught up. *Freedom.* I need to be free again, and this might be my last chance. My breaths come in pants as I sprint down endless corridors, through the archways and doors, down more stairs. I'm surprised to see no guards, no one watching me pass them. It's like I'm merely a shadow, a ghost of the girl held captive upstairs.

The darkness is my friend as I run through the maze of corridors until I come to a dead end and a single, massive stained red glass door. My heart is beating so fast as I walk to the door and touch the handle, letting it swing open. My bare feet make prints on the shiny floor as I step inside and let the door shut right behind me. A ballroom. At least, it was probably one, a grand ballroom at that, before time and neglect got its hands upon it. Now the shiny tiles are cracked, and the beautiful tapestries that line each wall, telling a story, are dusty and withered, parts of the cloth ripped and torn in places.

Moonlight shines in from the domed ceiling, but a lot of the glass is fractured, threatening to fall down on me. Do it, end this for me. Of course, it doesn't, and only the wind whistles through the fractures in answer to my thoughts. Even the wind sounds as lonely as I feel on the inside.

There's a giant chandelier hanging from the tallest part of the room, which must hold a thousand red diamonds, sparkling bright in silver moonlight, making this room surprisingly bright. The beauty of it distracts me. It distracts me from the nightmare that can't be real, distracts me from memories threatening to swallow me whole and from everything that I need distracting from before the sun rises tomorrow.

Breathless, I push away from the door and walk over into the centre of the room. I spin around in circles, my face lifted to the ceiling, and let the moonlight bathe me. When I pull my gaze back down again, my eyes fall upon mirrors tucked between each of the old tapestries. I stop spinning and look at my reflection trying desperately to claw through the thick layers of dust.

I can only blink as one of the mirrors moves to the side. I assume maybe it's an animal hiding in the shadows of the ballroom, but then Erax steps out, and my whole body freezes. He lets the mirror door swing back and close firmly in place behind him. It must have been some kind of secret passageway.

"Why are you not in your room, Mist?"

That nickname again. I clench my hands into fists and watch him lean against the mirror. For once, he is in casual clothes, which I have never seen him wear. A silky black shirt under a thick darker cloak, and soft dark grey trousers that hang low on his hips. Definitely not something I pictured him wearing. His dark hair is also unusually messy as if he just climbed out of his bed to chase me. I wouldn't put it past him. He'd probably enjoy the chase.

"Another secret part of this castle?" I ask, clearing my throat.

"There are tunnels everywhere. My grandfather was very keen that we could escape in the event of an attack." Like my parents didn't manage to do, he doesn't say, but the unspoken words are loud between us. His eyes widen slightly as they slowly roll down my body, making me hyperaware of any inch of my skin show-ing. My gold gown covers me from the neck down, but it stops at my upper thighs. "You should be in your room resting."

He looks away from me, and the heat I feel with his look goes with him.

"Why are you here? Is following princesses through castles a night job for you?" He chuckles low, blinking at me in surprise. I stop him before he can lie. "Let me guess, you have guards following me, told not to be seen—they were, by the way, every time. Not very good at hiding with all that armour on. You forget I grew up with guards following me. And nuns." I cross my arms. "The guards told you I tried to escape?"

His eyes reveal nothing. "Perhaps."

Huffing under my breath, I walk over to one of the tapestries for a much-needed distraction. It's a farmer's village, nothing more than fields and cows, the odd chicken. There's a blue light in the sky shining down on them, and it could be moonlight, but it's almost too blue, with not a drop of silver. I can't see what is above the light. That part is damaged. Deliberately, by the looks of it.

I feel Erax's eyes on me as I walk to the next one, briefly passing the mirror, catching his eyes in it. Even the flash of his eyes makes my heart race, but I put it down to anger and continue to the next tapestry. This one shows a castle built over farmlands, and there are very clearly dragons flying in the sky above them. A black fire grows in the distance.

"Who made these? What history is this?"

I don't recall seeing any of it.

Erax's voice is gruff when he replies. "I am not aware. No one alive is for that matter. Some parts of the castle were here before we built on it. My grandfather picked this area, and only he would know that answer." He glances around. "This is one of the older rooms. It needs renovating, but there hasn't been time." The next tapestries are even more confusing than the last. The farms are gone, and there are countless castles, guarded tall towers, and so many dragons that they fill the sky like a storm. They are all different colours, some that I've not seen before in the books I've read or the dragons I've seen fly the skies with their riders. The small black fire that had lurked in the distance now spreads over some of the grasslands.

"Why are you trying to run away from me?" The king's voice creeps over me like an unbidden caress. "Did you think I would let you go?"

"I wasn't running away," I snap at him. "I'm well aware the only way to escape you is death."

I don't tell him all of the truth—the nightmare, the feeling of being trapped that sent me running from my room. He would just laugh. I walk past the mirror to the next tapestry, my traitorous eyes looking for him. My skin pebbles when I notice he's only a few steps away from me, almost like he's hunting me. I never even heard him move.

I gulp as I look at the fourth tapestry. The dragons are burning the castle to ash. There's fire everywhere, this time flickering up in shades of red, orange, blue and green until it looks like a rainbow. The black flames are still there, but they're not as strong in this one. The middle and top of the tapestry are torn. I can only see bits of this story.

When I walk to the next part, all the way past the mirror, curious about what happens next, I almost jump when I realise he's right behind me. He's much closer now.

"Why were you running from me, Mist?"

I freeze, like a deer caught by a dragon swooping down over the forest. His deep, seductive voice all but breathes down my neck, sending shivers up my spine. "Wouldn't you like to know? Then you could use my weakness against me."

Turning around, I face him. I need to face him, to remember who he is and what he did. I lift my head as I do, making sure to look straight into his eyes that are flickering to gold around the edges. He steps into my space and pushes me against the mirror with his huge body, and I gasp.

"You are going to be my wife. Mine."

"I'm well aware," I breathe out. "Now let me go."

I'm barely able to get the words past my lips as I shove my hands into his chest. Erax grabs and holds them prisoner above my head, forcing my body to arch against his. We fit so perfectly together, and I hate it. I hate the way he looks at me. I hate the way my body *responds* to that look. I especially hate the way my pulse quickens when we're close like this. I just hate Erax so much. His name is another I will never forget. I have burned it too deeply into my memory.

"I wasn't finished, Mist. You are going to my bride, and anything that scares you is my weakness too."

I want to laugh at him. *You scare me. Spending the rest of my life with the man who killed my parents and then stole my kingdom from me scares me.*

"We will be married in title and nothing else," I say. "I don't love you. I will never love you." I peel my lips back in disgust, sneering at him. "You're a monster."

He laughs once, leaning into me, our lips only a breath away. "Have you ever been touched by a monster, Mist?"

My fast breathing causes my chest to brush against his, and my nipples peak with the movement. *It's anger, not arousal,* I tell myself over and over, like I can make it come true. I'm just so angry with him. Beyond angry. I want to hurt him like he hurt me.

He leans farther down, and when our eyes finally meet, his irises have bled away into pure gold. With him so close, I can't pull away. I can't even breathe without his scent filling my lungs. I hate how nice he smells too. Fire and roses is fast becoming a scent I search for in every room. I add his scent to my list of all the things I hate about Erax.

"If anyone has touched you, they are already dead. Tell me."

"No," I angrily growl at him.

He only leans more into me, our bodies completely flush. I can feel his hard cock pressing into my stomach, and heat builds between my thighs. I clench them to stop it, but nothing works. I don't understand why this is happening. Of all the betrayals I've faced in my lifetime, my body was never one of them. Why is it set on betraying me like this?

Why am I responding to Erax like he's my lover and not an enemy?

"What about with a man?" His voice is just above a whisper as he runs his fingers down the side of my throat. He pauses over my pulse and watches it flutter against him. "Answer me, Mist."

I twist and try to pull away again. He tightens his grip.

"I may not have done anything before," I gasp out, hating the moan that wants to build in the back of my throat, "but I've seen enough."

The priestesses weren't all virgins, and more than once, I walked in on things I wish I hadn't seen. Sister Gabriella was the worst of them. It was another way for her to humiliate me.

His lips tilt at the side, and there's a hint of amusement lacing his eyes that are turning back to green again. "So, the nuns were naughty, were they?" His fingers drift over my collarbone to the middle of my chest. They trail down until they reach the valley between my breasts, and his throat jerks as he looks at me, taking my body in. "I bet you used to spy on them."

I gasp when he touches my nipple and a bolt of pleasure shoots through me. Horrified by my reaction, I try to pull away again.

Erax digs his nails into my wrist, his gaze darkening. "Don't start acting shy with me now, Princess. I'm going to be inside a lot more of you than just your head starting from tomorrow." He slips a hand under my nightgown and slides it up my thigh. "Tell me the truth, Mist. Did you enjoy watching the nuns fuck each other? Did it make you wet..." He cups my sex and begins to tease me, his eyes never leaving my own. "Like you are now?"

I dip my head back and let out a moan. Gods, it's been so long since I let myself feel pleasure like this. I can't even remember the last time. Whatever he's doing feels much better than I used to do. Another moan escapes me. It's the sound of my moaning that seems to break me free of his spell, and I open my eyes, reality dawning on me again.

"*Let me go—now!*"

To my surprise, he does. Erax drops my hand and takes a step back from me, his arms crossed over his chest. He watches me for far too long before saying anything.

"I don't plan on hurting you, Mist. It doesn't really do anything for me. I want you to know that before tomorrow comes. Even if you drive me fucking insane, even if we are enemies that will never understand each other, or ever want to—I will keep you safe and never let anyone hurt you. You are my queen, and my protection is forever yours. Even if you don't want it."

His queen. Something about hearing those words makes the bond between us so final. So real. I pull away from the mirror, my legs shaking. However, as I take a step forward, my gown catches on the edge of the mirror, a single shard that must have broken on the corner, and I don't realise it's tearing until it's too late. Until the cool air caresses the skin on my back.

I immediately turn to face Erax, hoping he didn't see. I know by the look on his face that he saw my scars. There was no way he couldn't have caught a glimpse of them. My whole body tenses as he walks over. It is the first time I have ever seen his face pale. Yet there is a silent rage about him that bubbles beneath the surface. I can see it in his eyes, in the way he's walking towards me.

He stops in front of me and reaches out a hand. I immediately flinch and cover my head with my arms, an instinctive reaction I haven't felt since leaving the convent. When nothing happens, I lower my arms, surprised to find him staring down at me in surprise. His eyes have turned gold again, but for the first time ever, red specks flicker in them.

He drops his hand back by his side. "Show me."

Even though the command is quiet, the distinct harshness in his voice makes me shiver. His entire demeanour has changed. This isn't the Erax who tried seducing me a few moments ago. This is a king commanding me to obey him. And yet still I do not move. I can't. Because I don't want him to see. I don't want *anyone* to see what they did to me. The moment I show someone my scars, it makes what happened to me real, and I don't want what they did to me to be real. I just want to forget about it all.

"Maelena..." He whispers my name so softly it's like a plea. "Turn. Around."

Despite the warning laced in his voice, I shake my head. "I can't."

Please don't make me do this.

Even if I did want to show him, I'm completely frozen to the spot, barely able to breathe, let alone move my legs. Erax steps behind me. In one swift motion, he tears off the rest of my gown and lets it flutter to the ground next to me. For a painfully long moment, Erax says nothing. He just looks, and then he feels, touching, ever so gently, the scars on my back. My breath hitches with panic. I have never let anyone touch my back like this before. Not even Lochlan.

Erax moves his hand over my back slowly, tracing every scar as if mapping them out in his memory. I tense when he finds the most recent ones. Although they have mostly healed, the scars from my last night at the convent are still a little tender. A deep growl rumbles in his chest behind me.

"Who did this to you?" His voice is dangerously low and close, so close that his breath touches my neck and cheek. "Who the fuck did this to you? Tell me now!"

Tears slip from my lashes as my body trembles beneath his hand. "You know who did it."

You all knew—even the gods. Everyone chose to turn a blind eye to it. Even the gods when I begged them to stop it. To help me.

As if Erax would give a shit about my

scars anyway. They are just reminders of what he put me through. Because if he hadn't taken everything away from me, none of this would have happened, and my back would remain scarless. Instead, I carry them because of his doing, and he has the audacity to act like he cares? To pretend to feel sorry for me?

My tears turn into tears of rage. I wipe them with the side of my hand and glare up at him. "The priestesses told me how they were ordered to keep me in line, how you told them to do everything in their power to turn me into your perfect little princess bride. The punishments they gave me once a month, they were part of their so-called *training*"—I spit the last word out—"but I'm sorry you find my scars hideous to look at. The sisters healed what they could, of course, but I was told I only needed to lie on my back to please you, so you wouldn't see or care. As long as I could still open my legs for you, that was all that mattered."

I can barely see him through the tears rushing down my face when I open my eyes again. I don't bother wiping the tears away. He needs to see them. He needs to know.

"Who did this, Maelena?"

I turn around to face him and instil as much hatred as I can into my voice. "You did. Every scar, bruise and bone they broke in my body was carried out under your orders. Or so they said." He stares at my chest as if his eyes haven't moved since I turned around, as if he's still looking at the scars on my back. "If you think those are bad, they are nothing like the mental scars they gave me. Those will never heal. Sister Gabriella made sure of that."

Finally, he lifts his eyes to meet my gaze. They're almost completely red now, and his pupils have narrowed, reminding me of a serpent. A dragon. He suddenly whips his cloak off and drapes it over my shoulders. I leave his cloak on, knowing it's better than walking half naked back through the palace. Something heavy lies in the inner cloak pocket, and I pull it out, surprised to find my dagger survived. My father's crest is gone and has been replaced with a gold dragon, but the blade is still sharp and just as red. Erax must have had it mended.

Why would he fix a weapon that was used to try to kill him?

I look up to find him opening the mirror door again. The fact he's leaving after all I just said makes me want to throw my dagger at him. Maybe I'll have better luck from this angle. Maybe it will just satisfy me. Both outcomes are tempting.

"There are guards outside who will take you back," Erax growls.

He slams the door behind him, and I can only stare at my reflection as a horrible thought occurs to me. Why don't I feel relieved now that Erax is gone?

CHAPTER EIGHT

When the sun enters through my bedroom window, I close my eyes with a groan.

I can't believe it's morning already.

It feels like only minutes ago that the guards brought me back and I lay on this bed, thinking about how my life will end the moment that sun rises. Most of all, I thought about how I'll belong to the Dragon King and the kingdom he stole from me.

Now that the sun has risen, I don't think I can go through with it.

I turn on my side with another groan. My whole body feels like it's being weighed down by an anchor. Shame slowly creeps over me. The way Erax touched me last night... the way I *responded*... I have never felt something like that. These feelings are so different to the ones I feel for Lochlan. They're dark and heavy, like an unquenchable thirst rising from the pit of my stomach. A thirst that feels like it's drowning me the moment Erax touches my body.

I straighten up to sit on the edge of the bed, clutching the sides of the mattress. I would rather the gods strike me down than let me feel like this for him. I would betray not only myself and my parents, but all those who died because of him. I vowed long ago to never forget what he did to us. Last night in the ballroom, I almost did.

I almost let him devour me.

I can't let that happen again. Even if my body does respond to him, even if there is a tiny part of me in the darkest corner of my heart that does not hate him, I vowed to always be his enemy. And yet, last night we were almost... not that.

When Erax saw the scars on my back, he appeared shocked by them. Angry, even. I have spent all night thinking about his reaction. There was no way he could not have known. He was the one who put me there! He practically locked the door to my cage himself and then gave the nuns the key.

The sound of the door unlocking flips my stomach, and I immediately tense my shoulders, my chest tightening. I don't lift my gaze from the floor. I watch the rays of sunlight stretching over the hardwood, my chest tightening. When the door opens, a shadow eclipses the sunrays, and then a voice I did not expect to hear speaks.

"It's a little chilly in here, don't you think?" Noble's voice echoes around my room.

I frown at the shadow in the doorway. "What are you doing here?"

Noble leans against the wall, flashing me a grin. "You know, that's not usually what women say to me first thing in the morning. Have you frozen my irresistible charm as well as the lake?"

I shake my head with a laugh, trying to mask the fact I'm on the verge of a panic attack. As Noble walks towards me, the sun moves over him, reflecting off his green clothing. The rich green is a clear mark of his place in the wedding, and I have to admit, the suit is stunning. The woven material is the same shade as emeralds, with a gold collar and buttons. A green cloak falls from his shoulders, clipped with metal dragons in the same shade. There is the royal crest over his heart. The crest for my family should be here today, but I doubt I'll see it anywhere. He picks up the king's cloak from the bed. I hadn't realised I slept with it.

"You'll need this," he says, "and fireproof boots."

Erax's scent engulfs me as his thick cloak falls around my shoulders.

I hate that I don't hate that smell anymore. Damn fire and roses.

His smell.

Noble thrusts a pair of heavy boots into my arms, the same ones I use to wear around the castle. I can't help but wonder if he's going to help me escape. My heart jumps at the thought. Why else would he be here, alone, telling me to wear fireproof boots right before I'm to be married to his king? Of course, in the back of my head, I know the chances of him betraying his king are next to impossible. But I let myself believe it for a moment—that maybe, just maybe, there is a way out of this cage after all.

That there's still hope.

I slide my feet into the boots, fastening them quickly, but I'm still in my nightdress. "Where are we going?"

Noble doesn't answer. He just leaves the room, and my stomach flips again as I follow him out.

Outside in the corridors, servants rush by us, carrying large crates of wine and baskets of green and gold roses. They make my eyes sting as I pass them. Memories of my child-hood rush to the forefront of my mind. My mother loved gold roses because of how rare and difficult they were to successfully grow.

We used them for royal weddings too—as a symbol for new beginnings.

For me, they symbolise the end.

Once we are away from prying eyes, I again ask Noble, "Where are we going?"

He grins over his shoulder at me. "The king has brought something back for you. A gift. He wants to show you it before the wedding."

My gaze strays down to the floor. The king has brought something *back* for me. I frown at my reflection shining up at me. I don't want more gifts from him. I want answers—and revenge.

I was also a fool to think Noble would help me get out of here. He is clearly a loyal servant to his king.

When I lift my gaze from the floor, I'm met with a familiar entryway clouded by the smell of burning leaves hanging thick in the air. Noble arches his brow at me as he steps forward to open the crimson doors. I do not look at him when I pass through. Judging by his expression, I'm sure he knows I have been here before.

The waves of heat hit me again, instantly engulfing my senses. My eyes and throat begin to dry the farther we descend. The fire-proof boots help protect me from the hot ground, which is worse than it was in the tunnels I tried to escape in. The cloak protects me better, too. Only my face is exposed to the heat.

On the stair landing, I'm reminded of Erax and the moment he found me here. I had wanted so badly to kill him that night. I never imagined a few days later that I'd almost let him kiss me. It's like the gods are laughing at me now.

The air grows harder to breathe the closer we approach the bottom. When Noble steps out of the stairway and I follow him, I'm immediately aware of the intensity of the heat. Although it doesn't hurt me, I can feel its presence pushing against my boots. My feet would surely burn had I not followed Noble's instructions. I'm glad I did.

My eyes roam the dark walls around me. The black rock and low ceiling make me feel like I'm walking through a cave. I guess it would make sense that the dragons' keep would be hidden underground. As I trace unusual markings glowing within cracks in the wall, I glance at Noble as he leads the way down.

"I thought the wedding was taking place at dawn?"

"The king decided to postpone it," he says, "until noon when the sun is hottest. Don't worry, Ice Princess. You've still got a little more time to freeze the sun."

I let out a shaky breath. I don't know what I expected to feel in response to that, but it wasn't disappointment. No time to think about that. I've got until midday before I sign my life away. I want to enjoy every last moment of my freedom.

The dragons' keep is a massive cavern of lava, rivers and smooth rock. The elements seem to be combatting each other in nearly every inch of it, but it's the endless gaps in the cave, big enough for dragons, and the eyes I feel on me from the second I step in the keep. There are dragons hiding everywhere, lurking in the gaps and shadows, and I bet in the river that flows through the middle of the cavern, with a waterfall right at the back of the keep. Lava flows around the edges in its own rivers, and it pours down the stone like rain. I barely look at the rest of the cavern as my eyes drift to the king.

He isn't alone.

Although Erax faces our direction, his gaze is pinned on four individuals kneeling before him. His face is cloaked in shadows, but I know it's him. It's like his very essence is peering through the darkness to draw me in. My legs move forward of their own accord as if drawn to him. He doesn't look up at the sound of our footsteps approaching. If I could see him, I doubt he even blinked—too focused on those in front of him. One of them sways to the side with a whimper, as if they are struggling to hold themselves up from exhaustion or pain. I catch a glimpse of the shackles binding their wrists to their backs, and a feeling of ice-cold dread overcomes me.

Why have I been brought down here?

Once we have descended the last of the steps, Noble moves his hand to my shoulder and guides me around the platform. He places me on the far right of Erax. Despite still being widely out of his reach, I'm at least close enough to witness him stepping out into the sunlight. It pours down over him from the gap in the cavern right above us. Erax no longer smells just like fire and roses. A metallic tang hangs off him, and I don't need to look to know he is covered in blood. For a second, I panic, thinking it is his, but I soon realise it isn't.

I never expected my future husband to be covered in blood on the day of our wedding.

He looks just like he did when we met— silently unhinged, as if he's seconds away from burning everything around him to the ground. I follow his line of sight to the source of his contention, and the ground sways underneath me.

No, no, no. This can't be right.

Every fibre in my body recoils as the scars on my back tingle in memory of the pain I suffered all those long years.

This can't be real. You're *not real. None of you are!*

But the moment the sun hits them, I know they are real—as real as the night-mares that torment me most nights. As real as the scars they carved into my body and mind.

My very soul.

The four women kneeling before their king are as real as the hatred I have for them and have held onto since day one. That very hatred boils to the surface of my being at the sight of Sister Faye glancing back at me. I take a step back, vaguely aware of Noble steadying me with his hand on my shoulder again. Sister Breea and Sister Michael glance back at me too. I notice how all but one of the sisters is crying. If it weren't for the swelling of her face, I'd almost think she was smiling at me.

Shock and fear are the first emotions to fill me when I look at Sister Gabriella. Then comes the rage—the searing, blinding rage that rises from the depths of my body. To see her so beaten like this, kneeling before the very king she worshipped like a god all these years, brings me a sense of vindication I never thought I'd feel. My goal was always to escape her convent and never look back, but this?

This is poetic justice.

I can't take my eyes off her as she tilts her head up at her king. He removes his hands from behind his back to reveal a black object in his hands. My heart seizes when I run my gaze over it. Sister Gabriella's whip. The black handle gleams in the light as he glides his long fingers through the blood-stained tails. No matter how many times I was ordered to wash that whip, I could never get my blood out from its fibres.

Erax lifts his foot and places it on the rock, drawing my attention back to him. He rests his elbow on his knee and rotates the bottom of the whip, causing the handle to gleam against the sun. Its glare blinds me, and for a moment, all I can hear is his dangerously low voice echoing off the cave walls.

"An interesting tool, is it not?" He lifts the object up to the sun, the handle gleaming in the light. "That's what my grandfather used to call them: tools. He had a whole room dedicated to his collection of them, each one meticulously displayed." He grips the tails with his other hand and wraps them around his fingers. "One a month, when I was five, he would take me to that room and task me with polishing them. If I did a good job, I was rewarded. If I failed or knocked one of them over, he'd give me two lashes across the hand."

He pulls and strains the whip, then flicks it.

Snap.

Everyone jumps at the sound, including myself. His grandfather hurt him. Why would he hurt his heir? A few of the sisters whimper while another bursts into tears. I keep my eyes on Sister Gabriella. Although her expression is calm, not even she can hide the visible trembling of her shoulders. I watch as her fear slowly settles in. It claws at her throat, forcing her muscles to jerk and contract against her flesh, then it runs down her spine until her whole body trembles. As if to hide the wobbling of her chin, she rests it on her chest. But I saw it, and my heart skips a beat in surprise. I have never seen Sister Gabriella frightened before.

Angry, gleeful, smug—yes. But never afraid.

Erax stretches the tails to their full length, straining the leather. "Those lashes were nothing compared to what he did to the servants," he says, his voice sweeping over me again. "I can still hear their screams as they clawed at the chamber door, begging for death. There was barely any flesh on their bones once he was through with them." His eyes flick down to the sisters, taking in each of them slowly. "Do you know what it feels like to be whipped like that? No? What about you, Sister Faye? Or you, Breea?"

When at last his gaze lands on Sister Gabriella, Erax doesn't speak.

He strikes.

—SLASH—

The whip whooshes down over the side of her face. Her head snaps to the side from the impact, but she does not make a sound, not even when the tip of the tail catches her left eye and blood seeps through her swollen lids. Erax strikes her again and again, and each time the whip contacts a different part of her body. His movements are expert. Concise. This isn't the first time Erax has used a whip. I can tell by the utter precision of his blows and the way he angles his wrist. But while Sister Gabriella had always looked disgusted when she did this to me, Erax appears to be enjoying it. There's a manic look in his eyes that reminds me of a predator rabidly tearing into its prey. I want to stop him or join him. It scares me that I don't know which.

I want to grab that whip from his hands

and destroy it once and for all. Burn it to ash so that its existence is no longer. But I can only stand frozen as memories of my own torture rush to the forefront of my mind. My throat dries and the air around me grows thicker as I dig my nails into the centre of my palms, recalling the brutal way that whip had torn my body and soul to pieces. By the tenth brutal strike, Sister Gabriella finally cries out.

"Spare me, please!"

"Did you spare my wife?!" Erax snarls as he lunges at her. He drags her up to her feet by the hair and dangles her old, tiny frame off the ground above him. "I ordered you to protect your future queen at all costs!" He digs his fingers into her windpipe. "You were to keep her safe from... the fucking curse and the witch assassins they sent."

What is he saying? I was his prisoner. His *property*. He said so himself. Yet, he's talking about me as if he actually cared about how I was treated at the convent. As if I had meant more to him. What does he mean by witch assassins??

"F-forgive me, my king... I was trying...

to... tame her," Sister Gabriella chokes between strangled breaths, her features twisted in anguish. "For you, my king!"

"I did not order you to tame her." Erax spits each word out slowly. "I ordered you to protect her. You are a traitor, Gabriella, and you know what I do with traitors in my kingdom. I feed them to my dragon."

Despite struggling to breathe, Sister Gabriella breaks down and begins to wail. "N-no! Show me mercy, my king... Please, show me mercy!"

Erax snarls into her face, his lips peeled back in disgust. "Where was my wife's mercy?"

For some reason, seeing her crying and begging for mercy like I did so often during my punishments makes me feel sorry for her. It's like I'm seeing her for the old woman she always was, one that hid behind the power of her whip. Now she looks frail dangling from the king's grasp. Fragile, even. I want to turn away from her, but instead I take a step forward.

"Don't," Noble whispers in my ear. "Just watch. Have faith in your king."

Noble hardly gives me a choice. He places his hand on my shoulder again, but his grip is a touch too firm. I stay still, my head swimming with so many thoughts and memories and truths I never expected to hear. All this time, I thought I was placed in the convent as discarded property, left there for Sister Gabriella and her acolytes to torture me. To find out now that Erax hid me there to keep me safe from the witches? I thought the witches were extinct, or at least, that's what my mother once told me. She also told me they were the original protectors of the dragons and helped breed them... why would they want me dead? What curse??

Erax looks at me for the first time since coming here, and my heart stills. The manic look that had gripped him only moments before has been replaced with a rage so boiling it sears the air around me.

"What would you have me do to them?"

My breath catches, burning in the back of my throat. He's asking me what *I* want to do? He just stated there's already protocol when it comes to traitors. My parents had sent our traitors to the Citadel for the Grand Masters to deal with. Depending on the severity of their crime, most of them were trained to work there as servants under the promise of one day earning back their freedom. Something tells me the same mercy is not given to traitors in Erax's kingdom. Not by the look in his eyes.

I glance back at the sisters sobbing on the ground behind me. One of them has fainted. In all the years they dragged me to that awful chamber, they never once showed me mercy. It was clear from the beginning they enjoyed what Sister Gabriella put me through. And yet they look so traumatised by all this that I find it hard to believe they would be stupid enough to ever do it again. I also believe that if I don't show mercy now, then I'm no better than them. You can't fix a broken world by continuing to chip away at it.

"Let them go," I say. "They won't hurt anyone again. If they do, we'll know about it, because our eyes are everywhere. Is that not right, Sister Gabriella?"

She somehow manages to nod whilst clawing at her captor's hand.

Erax throws Sister Gabriella to the

ground. As he watches her gasp for breath before him, her frail body crumpled and covered in blood, a dark smirk works its way slowly over his lips.

"You are lucky the gods blessed you with a merciful queen," Erax says. "The same cannot be said for your king." He steps back, his cloak billowing. "Cyrsí... *Ignisin.*"

A rush of hot air sweeps over me, dragging my hair over my shoulders and lifting the bottom of my dress. From the shadows, a beast I'm all too familiar with slowly reveals itself. At first, only its eyes are perceptible, burning like twin pools of molten lava. But then its chest begins to glow as fire builds and shines through its bristling scales. Erax looks at his dragon proudly.

"Cyrsí has been off her food lately," he says, his smile twisting into a cruel sneer, "but something tells me that's about to change."

My voice dies in the back of my throat as the dragon lowers its head, and the horns on the side of her face bristle as a loud rumble reverberates around the keep. The fire in her chest builds, glowing brighter. Her eyes never leave Sister Gabriella, who is whimpering at her mercy. I know why Erax is doing this. As a king he has no other choice —by defying his orders they committed treason against him. He's not doing this just for me but for him too. He looks at his dragon, and then nods once.

Cyrsí turns her attention to the other sisters. I watch in horror as she steps forward, causing the ground to tremble under her weight. I'm too stunned to blink let alone move. I should say something to stop him and yet... I can't move. Deep down there's a part of me that doesn't want to spare their lives. After all the horrific things they did to me and countless others, they deserve this. Don't they?

"But she is the enemy," one of the acolytes cries out. I can't see who, but it sounds like Sister Michael. "We did only what was asked of us!"

"What Sister Gabriella commanded us to do!" Now, that voice I do recognise. Breea. She was the one who hauled me out of bed before dragging me to the room. "Please show mercy, my king, if not for us, then for those who were bent against our will!"

Erax doesn't move. He watches his dragon open its mouth, revealing the searing fire that has gathered inside. I can feel its heat from where I'm standing. He gives Noble a quick, barely noticeable glance, and it's then Noble tries to take me away. I still can't seem to move my legs. I can only watch as Erax gives a final command, and his dragon releases her horrid black fire breath. Sister Breea's wailing screams echo around me as she's burned alive in black flames that sparkle like stars in the night sky. Nothing remains of her but a pile of ash on the ground.

Erax gives the command again, and his dragon moves on to the next victim. All the while, Sister Gabriella screams and wails as she watches them die, knowing she will come last. Noble tries again to pull me away, but I shrug him off, oddly compelled to see it through.

"The king does not—"

"I want to watch," I tell him.

He looks over at Erax, who nods once

before turning his attention back to his beast. The dragon works its way through each of the sisters, leaving nothing of their existence behind but the same pile of ash. Then it moves to Sister Gabriella. It lifts its head, pausing as it looks down at her, its chest burning with more fire breath. Sister Gabriella doesn't move or try to scramble away like the others. She looks the dragon in the eye and accepts her fate with a surprising courage I can't help but admire even though I hate her. Sister Gabriella is the only one the dragon doesn't burn completely, choosing to eat her instead while she's still alive and screaming in her mouth.

"Now I'm ready," I say, turning to Noble.

As he leads me away, I glance back at the king, who's watching me with a smirk on his face. To my surprise, and perhaps a little to my horror, I feel no pity or remorse for those he just killed in my name. I feel only relieved.

At least, for a moment I do.

I still have the wedding to get through.

CHAPTER NINE

From today, my life belongs to the Dragon King and the kingdom he stole from me.

I barely remember Noble escorting me back to my room after the dragons' keep before I got back into bed, exhausted and drifting to sleep. I can't think about anything else as I'm dragged out from my bed while the sun shines outside the window. The very window I've thought about jumping from more than once. I no longer voice my protests to any of the servants. I'm bathed by them, twice, before the maids deem me satisfactory, and then I'm shoved into a stunning gold gown.

I never knew what I'd wear on my wedding day, never thought about it, and I hate to admit that this dress is gorgeous.

Two pure gold dragons curl around my breasts in a bodice, meeting in the middle, and their eyes are fire red rubies. They are a shade darker gold than the rest of the dress, which is layers of silk, satin, chiffon and so much detail in each layer that I can't help but wonder who made this. A thin layer of chiffon falls over my upper arms in three waves, and each wave has a dragon crest matching the rest. It's beautiful, but I know my mother, who should be here, would hate it. She used to spin me around in my red dresses as a little girl, telling me when I marry, my dress would be like hers on her wedding day. Red, for our kingdom, for my father's crown.

The stylist finishes my hair, leaving most of it down in waves except for two braids that pull my locks from my face and, no doubt, are to help the crown sit comfortably on my head. Nothing about today will make me comfortable. Light makeup is covering my cheeks, but as I was told is their tradition, two gold dragons have been stencilled and painted underneath my eyes, just where my tears will fall. "Princess, you look beautiful. You will make a lovely queen."

I smile tightly at the maid. She doesn't know I hate the king and want none of this. That this may be a wedding celebrated across the kingdom, but for me, it might as well be a funeral. "Thank you."

"Leave us!" I turn as a woman enters my room through the open door, and the maids hurry out in a rush. Whoever she is—they listen to her. The familiar woman is very pretty, with classical features, bow lips and long blonde hair that hits her waist, longer than mine. She slowly looks me up and down, even though we are the same height, disgust flashing in her eyes before she smiles like a cat. "My name is Ambre. My father, your uncle, told me to come and offer you friendship on your big day."

There is so much sarcasm dripping from her words that I'm sure not even an idiot would believe her. Ambre, that's why she is familiar. "I know you. Uncle Dasinth told me stories of his daughter. I wasn't aware you lived in the castle."

"I was invited here as a guest." She

touches one of the many necklaces spread out on my bed on a silver cloth, waiting for me to choose one. The maids said Erax had each of them made for me, one of many gifts I'm supposed to receive. I don't want any of them. "You can have one if you like."

She picks up a choker of a gold dragon and walks to me, her tight black dress brushing the tiles. "You should wear this one. Fitting, for a slave labelled a queen."

"What do you want, Ambre?" I question, taking the choker from her hand. "You don't like me; I can see that. I don't know what I did to piss you off, but I'm really not in the mood to deal with you today. Uncle Dasinth was wrong to send you here. Where is he?"

Ambre turns and walks to the door. "You're not really our family, so why would he be here today? I'm sure he has better things to do." She stops at the door, looking back at me. It stings that he isn't here. He might not be blood, but I've always seen him as family. "I came to see if you'd be any competition for me when it comes to the king. He needs you for an heir to settle the kingdom, but after? You won't be needed, and he will find much more interesting companions to turn into his queen."

My heart races as something burns in my chest. I can't name the feeling that is clawing up my chest, but it's there and it isn't going away as I watch her. "And your conclusion?"

She sweetly laughs, meeting my eyes. There is nothing but spite in her gaze and a longing for the crown, a sight I've seen in a thousand faces when they look at me. "I have nothing to worry about. Congratulations, Your Majesty. May your marriage be fruitful sooner rather than later."

Bitch. Where is a dragon to eat her?

Ambre slams the door shut behind her, and I flinch. Another enemy in this forsaken castle! I throw the stupid necklace at the wall, and it cracks in two before falling to the floor. Two maids rush into the room, both their eyes widening at the broken necklace. "If that one isn't to your liking, may we suggest one of the other—"

"I'm not wearing any of them." I push past them both to stand in front of the door, where my shoes are waiting. I'm going to be queen soon, and there is nothing I can control about today, but I'm not wearing one of the necklaces that feel like chains. I can control this at least.

I slide my feet into small gold heels, and I'm barely able to walk in them as I step back. Before leaving, I glance at myself in the mirror, knowing no matter how pretty I look, my father would be ashamed of me and so would my mother.

They would have rather killed me than let me marry their enemy.

But they're not here, and I have to make a life for myself. I have to fight for myself. No one else is going to.

One more time, I allow my gaze to drift to the open window and the peace it offers. Death or marriage? A ray of sunlight shines over my pillow, where the dagger is hidden underneath. He was kind and promised not to hurt me. I'm not sure I can trust his promise, but the dagger... the dagger, I can trust. It felt different, like a lifeline being thrown to me when I was drowning.

Before I can do anything, the maids are ushering me out of my room. I have to hold up the ends of my dress so I don't trip on it as I am quickly taken through the heavily guarded castle, and I'm shoved into a carriage waiting outside. I barely get a second to take in my surroundings before the carriage is riding through the crowded streets, full of screaming, cheering, adoring people. Children race after the carriage, throwing what looks to be gold petals. I can barely see through them to look at the actual city as they rain down the carriage windows.

It feels like only minutes before we are driving by the cathedral. It's a beautiful, old building with weathered grey stone and stained glass windows of gold and red. I'm surprised when we go past it and down another packed street of people that look richer by the condition of their dresses and suits.

Most of them are clapping and cheering, but a good amount of them are leering and watching the carriage move by. There are so many men watching and waiting, and I sink back in my seat, away from their gazes. I remind myself that I am not wholly welcome here. My supporters might be hidden somewhere among the crowds, but it's clear those leering at me are not them.

The carriage stops outside another chapel. This one is smaller than the other. The door is opened and I climb out. Immediately, two guards are at either side of me. They guide me down the gold walkway to the chapel, where I'm led inside to a massive prayer room. The guards remain at the door, and I glance at the two priests waiting at the back of the small room. One is as old as time, so wrinkled that I barely see how he's still standing in his white robes. The other is a priestess, not one I know, but they all look the same to me. Stern, bitter women. They both bow when I stop in front of them. The priestess wrinkles her nose. "Are you aware of our rituals, Princess?"

I clear my throat and clamp my shaking hands together in front of me. "No."

I don't bother adding her title. I'm so sick of seeing priests and priestesses.

The priest looks at my hands before stepping forward. "You are safe, Princess. Please do not be scared. Of course you wouldn't know. My name is Priest Jean." He places his hand on my shoulder. His voice is softer than the woman beside him. "It is an honour to meet you, Princess Maelena."

I resist the urge to knock his hand off me despite his kindness. "Likewise." I don't bother hiding the sarcasm in my voice. "Why am I here? Shall we just go to the chapel and get it done quickly?"

"Impertinent, spoiled princess!" the priestess snaps at me, clutching her walking stick tightly. "I had been warned but never imagined—"

"Oh, she is simply eager to marry our king," the priest cuts in, "which can only be expected. He is very handsome, and the union of our kingdoms will bestow upon us great fruition." Just when I think the priest might not be so awful, he ruins it by mentioning that. It's clear the joining of our kingdoms is a union I want no part of. "I am afraid you must remove your lovely dress, Princess. You may have it back after the ritual, when you are married to the king and your union consummated."

"*What*?" I whisper in disbelief, sickness

rising in my throat. "But it took forever to get into it."

I can't help but laugh at my own response. Of course, that really wasn't what I wanted to say. What I want to say is—*are you fucking serious?* These people are sick if they are.

The priestess takes a step closer. "The future queen must be fully seen by the kingdom. It is a tradition that goes back hundreds of years. All noble women do this. I am afraid it must be the same for you. You are to walk through the crowds in nothing but your skin for the gods to see so that they might wash any sins that cling to your body. It is to make you completely pure. You understand this must be done."

It isn't a question. It's a demand.

Two priestesses step forward and walk towards me from opposite sides of the room, blocking me in. I take several steps back, almost stumbling over the dress. "Absolutely not!" I hold my hands out to them. "Don't you come anywhere near me. Do not touch me!"

"Come here, you insolent child!" the priestess shouts as I continue stepping back.

The other two priestesses go to grab my arms, but I lurch away from one, only to trip on the dress and fall with the other tightly grabbing my wrist. Someone catches me before I hit the ground. I look up to see Erax frowning down at me, his arm around my waist, his eyes burning with something dark and dangerous.

"I would suggest you take your hands off her before you bruise my future queen." Erax doesn't look at them when he speaks. He keeps his eyes locked on me, and his scent is like a comforting wave as it washes over me. "Or this will not end well for either of you."

The priestesses immediately let me go and jump back as if shocked by his words. My cheeks burn as Erax straightens me, and I step out of his arms the moment I can. My heart races as he looks at me slowly, a dark, primal desire burning in his eyes. It seems like he needs more than a minute before he can pull his gaze away towards the others waiting.

I look at him too, shocked. The black

scaled leather clothes are gone, replaced with dark green and gold fine clothes that are tightly fitted to his toned body. A gold cloak falls from his shoulders, and his black hair is styled rather than the usual windswept way he wears it.

He looks like a king about to marry a princess of an enemy kingdom.

He looks like the kind of man I would have begged my father to let me marry.

He looks like someone I want as mine.

"What is going on here?" he demands of them. They all look between each other, but there is no mistaking the venom in his tone. "Do not make me repeat myself. Speak, or I will drag the words out from you myself!"

The priestess quickly explains about the tradition that takes place before the ritual, apparently one his great-grandmother went through.

"It is tradition, Your Majesty," the priestess concludes. "The gods demand it be so."

Erax clenches his fists. "Do you think I'm a fool? The ritual has not taken place in generations." He glares at the priestesses moving ever so slightly forward, possibly to get away. It's unclear. "Touch my wife again and I will kill you in front of your gods."

The older priestess splutters something unintelligible, then again tries to justify her actions. "My king, the ritual is needed for such a sinful queen—"

He interrupts her with a snarl. "Fuck the ritual! Only I get to see what is under my wife's dress. She. Is. Mine!" No one dares to argue with him again or challenge the downright possessiveness of his statement. "Now go to the chapel to wait for us, and while you are at it—run. I won't be expected to wait for you, old man. I will walk my bride there myself. In her dress. Is that clear?"

They each nod and bow their heads, although somewhat hesitantly.

Noble stands a few feet away from us, and I don't notice him until he speaks. "Now, when the king, who rides a fucking dragon, tells you to run... *run*."

They scurry away, each breaking into a run. Noble moves into the path of the oldest priestess, stopping her. Erax looks at me as he tells her, "Not you, priestess. You're to go with us riders."

"But, my king—"

He looks over at her, his face impassive. "I believe you were a regular guest at where my princess grew up?"

"Well, yes," she begins, confusion making her eyebrows rise. "I can't see how that—"

Erax's tone holds no time for her. "Then you go with my riders." I'm confused as I look at them all. The priestess leaves with Noble and two other men I've not seen before, clearly more of the king's riders from their leather clothes and casual stance. Erax's eyes seem to flicker down my dress more than once, making me feel extremely nervous, before he offers me his elbow. *I wonder what he thinks.* "Come, we have quite a bit of a walk. The carriage already left, or I would ask for it to take us."

"As long as I can keep my dress on, I'm happy," I answer, still confused that he stopped it from happening. *He helped me again.* "Wait a second." I lean down, taking the heels off my already blistered feet and chucking them to the side. "I'm sorry, but I can't walk all that way in those heels."

He smirks at me, and then he laughs. I can't help but chuckle slightly with him, which seems to take him by surprise. It surprises me too. For a moment, it feels like the weight of the kingdom isn't on our shoulders as we walk. That we aren't enemies, and this isn't the man who killed my family and took my throne from me. He's just a beautiful man I'm about to marry.

Of course, reality is a bitch, and it knocks me off my feet within seconds the moment we exit the small chapel. I look away from him, reminding myself of my fate. Erax seems content to do the same as we step out into the crowds. Guards line the streets now, standing in front of the crowds of people and not letting them pass. They throw gold petals over us as we continue to walk, and Erax doesn't say a word to me.

Is he as nervous as I am? Isn't this everything he wanted? Or is he unhappy with the idea of marrying me too? I should feel relieved at the prospect, but there's a part of me that is shockingly disappointed. And I don't like how that part of me keeps growing bigger.

My eyes flicker out across the people, some of whom must remember my parents as they cheer and support the celebration. I can't help but be amazed at how there isn't an ounce of fear on their faces. They adore this man, this usurper who took everything from me. But the people look better than I remember them as a child, less thin and sick. They all seem to have colour in their cheeks and a happiness in their eyes I never witnessed until now. Why did they never look like this when my parents ruled?

Did my parents not look after their people like they swore they would? I was very rarely allowed outside the castle grounds. In fact, I can count on one hand how often I visited the people of our kingdom. I remember their condition being poor during difficult harvests, but I never realised how bad until now. I have so many questions taking root in my mind, but I know this isn't the day for them.

When we reach the cathedral, I immediately feel so nervous that sickness rises in my throat. A dragon roars above us the moment my bare feet step onto the cold marble steps, and flames lick the skies. Erax's dragon swoops over the chapel, followed by ten other dragons in shades of red and orange, and they fly high above, circling the chapel. They swirl around each other, diving and spinning, and it's stunning to see.

"Are they dancing?" The question escapes me as I watch them. I have heard of dragon dancing, but I wasn't sure it was true. I certainly never imagined I'd get to see it one day, let alone on the day of my wedding.

"Yes," Erax answers. "They are happy. It is an honoured wedding gift for us."

We watch them for a few more minutes, and tears well in my eyes. It's like they're dancing to a song only they can hear, and how I wish I could hear the lyrics for just one moment. With a gentle pull, Erax leads me into the chapel. His boots echo on the dark stone and braziers flicker as we pass by them. The building seems to have been carved out of gorgeous red trees that cover the walls and stretch all the way up to the vaulted ceiling. Gold leaves litter every inch of the floor, sparkling in the sunlight which shines through the many gaps in the walls.

There are statues of the gods here, behind the altar. A black onyx statue for Nytar, and a red ruby statue for Hekai. They stand tall and imposing, their hands wielding dragons like weapons, and they look down at us as if we are vermin. At least that's how I've always felt these gods look whenever they are depicted. Their expressions certainly don't make me ever want to pray to them.

Erax doesn't stop walking until we are fully inside the building, away from all the eyes of the outside crowds. A lone priest stands by the altar, waiting for us. The old man who told me to strip not so long ago. My blood boils at the sight of him. I am surprised, however, to find the rest of the room is empty. There are no witnesses, no servants. Just this man and the one beside me who is about to claim me as his wife.

"Where's everyone else?" I ask, my voice barely a whisper.

Erax leans down, his hot breath caressing my ear. "Our ritual is for us. I cannot give you privacy in other ways, like a normal woman might have, but it is in my power to give you this."

I blink twice in pure surprise. I thought he'd want every noble in his kingdom to attend the wedding. To witness the final *fuck you* to my father as he takes me as his bride, securing his reign once and for all. I didn't expect this kind of mercy.

"Where was my wife's mercy?"

My cheeks flush at the memory of his words, at the way he avenged me. Soon we are both standing in front of the priest, who goes over the ancient binding words that will link our lives together. Most are in a language I do not know, and I try to keep my hands from shaking as his chant rolls down my spine. For all I know, he could be binding my soul to the king's forever, in this realm and the after realm, and there is nothing I can do about it. But then, isn't that exactly what we are doing here? The moment I become the king's wife, our souls will be bound for eternity.

While I watch the priest, deaf to whatever he is saying, Erax keeps his eyes locked on me, never leaving my face for one moment. Once the priest is finished speaking his strange tongue, he offers him a dagger. Erax cuts a line down his palm without blinking.

"Here, make a cut." He hands me the white dagger, stained in his blood. "Make an offering to the gods so they might bless our union."

I stare at the dagger for far too long, my eyes stinging with unshed tears, wondering if I should press the blade into my chest and die or marry my enemy. I think to kill myself now would be a cowardly way out of this, and wouldn't that just give him what he wants deep down? He's only marrying me out of duty to his kingdom and to uphold his reputation.

Besides, I've come to realise that I'm not ready to die. Not yet. I need more out of my life. I *want* more, and I'm willing to fight for it, even if that means fighting my husband for the rest of my life.

I run the dagger across my palm, wincing at the sharp sting as my blood pours down my hand, and I close my fingers. Erax takes my hand in his, fusing our cuts together, our bloods mixing in an eternal bond of fire and roses. I swear fire and ice flash in our joined hands for a second, but I blink and it's gone. Did he see that? Did anyone?

The priest clears his throat. "Do you wish to repeat the vows after me—"

"No," Erax murmurs, his eyes intent on me. "I know them."

He tugs me closer, our hands held so tight, and for a second there is just us. Two people standing before the gods, lying to them that we aren't enemies but lovers who want to be married, and Erax is the most beautiful liar of all. He looks into my eyes as if searching for something, as if he's stripping every layer of my courage away, down to my very soul. I feel naked under his gaze, and I'm shivering.

"I stand before the gods, before the sun, moon and stars, to pledge my soul to you, Maelena." He lifts his injured hand and presses it over my heart, his blood seeping through my dress, then he smears his thumb down my lips, and I can taste it. Our blood joining together, our soul binding to each other. "Take my blood as your power and my body as your shield, and I will be the vessel that carries you. I will protect you and honour your needs and satisfy your every desire. I alone will worship your body, for you are mine, and I am yours." He gently cups my cheek, smudging the dragons. "Mine."

That word takes my breath away.

The priest has me repeat the vows, and then Erax pulls me to him and kisses me. His lips are like a branding, far worse than the vows of our marriage, far worse than our blood mixing together, because when he kisses me, he possesses me down to my very core. He consumes me with every second of his lips pushing against mine, every inch of his skin brushing my body as his hand slides down to my neck, pulling me closer together like he can't get enough. Like I'm the very air to his lungs. The truest worst thing of all... is that I don't want him to stop.

When he breaks away, loud bells ring across the city, and the cheering can be heard even louder than the bells. Even louder than my racing heart. With nothing but gold in his eyes, he steps back but links our hands. I'm too shocked to pull away.

"I have a present for you, my wife, to celebrate our marriage."

"I don't need more gifts," I say, letting go of his hand, feeling cold when I'm not in his arms anymore.

He shrugs a shoulder. "Humour your husband and come see it anyway. You might change your mind."

Husband.

Erax walks to the back of the chapel. Curiosity compels me to follow him. Outside, in the well-maintained gardens, three bonfires have been lit. Thick, black smoke stretches into the sky where the dragons are still dancing. Their giant forms briefly eclipse the sun. My blood runs cold as I look over each of the bonfires. They aren't empty. People have been burned in them. I recognise a few of the charred, blackened corpses still tied to the logs, and a wave of nausea hits me.

Erax places his hand on my back. "You remember your protectors—all the nuns I ordered to look after you? All the people who witnessed or took part in your torture?" He follows my gaze, and a smile lights up his face. "Their bodies will line the streets as my gift to you."

My mouth parts. I don't know how to feel —happy or horrified. Definitely both. And I definitely should not be surprised Erax would do something like this after what he did to Sister Gabriella and her acolytes. But still... Is this what revenge feels like? It tastes more bitter than sweet.

Erax watches me, gauging my reaction carefully, a hopeful glint in his eye.

"Dead, burnt bodies aren't a gift, Erax."

"To a dragon, they are." He leans in, kissing my cheek. He killed them, all of them, who hurt me and played a part in my decade-long torture. There were at least fifty of them. I still don't know how to feel. "No one is ever going to hurt you and think they will get away with it. You're my wife, Maelena. My queen. Now let's go celebrate."

CHAPTER TEN

I have always known I would be queen one day.

I just never thought I'd be the queen of my enemy's kingdom.

Erax's kingdom. The way he called me his queen sent shivers racing through my body, igniting every pore and scar with a desire I've been too frightened to feel.

The excitement is palpable in the air the moment we exit the cathedral. I squint against the blinding sunlight reflecting off the rows of golden armour lined up outside. Beyond the wall of guards framing the pathway, thousands of people have gathered behind them to celebrate, and they're all cheering and throwing confetti. Gold petals cascade around us, some of them landing on our heads and shoulders. I smile at the white sunflower seeds being tossed alongside them, scattering over the ground at my feet. It was tradition in my parents' kingdom to throw the seeds at newlyweds to wish them good luck in their marriage.

Newlyweds.

The word stops me in my tracks. Erax — my *husband*—glances at me. Is that apprehension or annoyance on his face? My hand throbs, and I rub it absentmindedly, my fingers brushing the cut that bound us to each other. It pulses under the bandage Erax wrapped around my hand before we stepped outside. He watches the movement and then, to my surprise, takes my hand in his injured one. Once more joining us.

I hold my breath as I let him lead me down the path to the carriage waiting for us. He waves to his people—to *our* people. I glance up at their faces peering around and over the guards, trying to get a glimpse of us. Children poke their hands through the legs of the guards to throw more confetti. I raise my free hand, and I wave at them all.

They return the gesture with even louder cheers and even more applause. Somewhere amongst these people are assassins and people who want to hurt me. I allow myself just a moment to forget about that. It's not every day a woman gets married to the enemy of her life.

Besides, the dragons flying low overhead and the hundreds of guards forming a protective wall around us are surely enough of a deterrent for now. At least I hope so.

At the end of the path, Erax helps me into the carriage. He then climbs in and slides onto the seat beside me instead of the one across. I stare at the empty seat, my whole body tensing as it instantly begins to heat up. We're so close to each other. Far too close. His scent engulfs me, mingled with the smell of his blood on my lips and the memory of the kiss we shared as man and wife. Man and wife. The reality is like a heavy fog wrapping around my senses until they've been completely devoured by him, and all I can think about are those three things. His scent, his blood, and that awful kiss that bound me to him and made me weak at the knees.

He taps the roof, and the carriage jolts into motion. The sound of the seeds pelting off the carriage reminds me of rain tapping against a windowpane, and for some reason it makes me smile. I always liked the sound of rain. Even on stormy nights, I found its presence to be comforting. Grounding. However, in the corner of my eye, I spot Erax watching me, as if scrutinising my smile, and it makes me uncomfortable. My cheeks flame.

Why, now, am I suddenly feeling embarrassed with him?

No, not embarrassed.

Shy, as if I'm just a girl again, with a stupid little crush on the boy who always tried to look out for her at the convent. I shake my head. Husband or not, Erax is still my enemy. The convent suddenly feels like another lifetime. I can't let myself forget it. I scoot as close as I can to the window and focus on the people cheering outside. No, I can never let myself forget what he did that day he burned my world to the ground.

It feels like only minutes pass before the carriage arrives. It halts outside the palace doors, and I'm relieved to see no more nun-eating dragons or bodies being burned alive.

I think I've had my fill of that. I don't want any more gifts from the king.

As I let him take my hand and help me out of the carriage, I can't help but wonder if that *is* what he's doing—making amends via these gifts—and why. I thought he hated me.

I thought *I* hated him.

But the way my ridiculous heart is beating right now makes me wonder that perhaps I don't hate him as much as I once did. Perhaps neither of us do. Or, and this is highly likely, perhaps he's just trying to lull me into a false sense of ease so I'll let my guard down. Then, when I least expect it, he'll attack again. My heart doesn't seem to want to believe that. It's still beating like a star shooting across the sky at hypersonic speed.

Erax climbs out of the carriage first and then again offers me his hand. I slide my own tentatively into his. His grip is surprisingly firm as he leads me back into his home. Behind us, his people wait in anticipation at the gates. It had been customary in our kingdom to allow those wishing to celebrate the royal wedding into the palace where they would be invited to feast and enjoy the festivities. However, the guards are ordering everyone to return home.

"Why are you not letting them in?"

Erax pulls me after him, his strides long and hurried. "I want the feast to be an intimate one. Close friends and members of my court only."

"Don't you trust your people?" I ask.

"Do you trust *our* people?" he retorts, with a light emphasis on the word *our*.

I glance back at the palace doors closing behind us. Even when this kingdom was my home, I could never trust everyone in it. Now that this kingdom—my *home*—is bonded to another one that quite clearly wants nothing to do with me, even if their disdain is subtle, I can only imagine how much greater at risk I am here.

Erax approaches the great hall quickly and confidently. The doors are opened for him, and he leads me inside, his hand still tethered to my own.

The room has already been filled with tons of people, but I'm too busy taking in the stunning decor to pay them attention. Gold paper dragons blow in the breeze across the ceiling, with silk ribbons falling from them and stopping just above our heads. The tables are all matching with gold plates, cloths and glasses, but it's the orbs filled with soft gold light lining the edges of every table that really make it feel magical in here.

My eyes land on the two thrones raised on a high dais in front of the spectacular window. I have my own one now, and it looks just like the king's except it's white instead of black. The thrones are dragons themselves, curled around a seat. The tails of the dragons are wrapped together in the middle of the two thrones.

I climb the dais with Erax, who stands to address everyone. I recognize none of them except for Noble, who is front and centre, his tall, lean body draped in a green cloak with gold buttons and embellishments. He looks so regal. Noble, even.

I fight a smile as I turn to face the people in front of me. A strange part of me wishes that I could find a familiar face. I know I should be totally against this marriage. The mere thought of wanting to celebrate it makes me feel sick, and yet... and yet there's a part of me that wants to. The same part that cannot forget the kiss we shared and the words he said to me in that cathedral. It's like they're poisoning my mind, taking root at the very depths of my being.

"Since the beginning of our world, our kingdoms have never known true peace. We are a people built and bred in war, for war and to die in nothing but fire and blood. Today marks the end of this endless cycle as we unite our lands in one kingdom. I fought and bled for each of you here today, and many of you stood proudly at my side, and now I have my wife. The queen wants the same as I. In the name of the gods we all worship, may today begin a rule of peace."

He nods at me, and we both settle into our thrones. I place my hands on the armrests, feeling the smoothness of the stone and leather seats. I blink at Erax suddenly reaching for my hand and holding it, his own now draped over the space between us just to touch me. The dance my heart gives is equally as gut wrenching as it is exhilarating.

A servant offers me a glass of wine, but I

shake my head. I've never tasted wine before —the smell always made me gag when the sisters made me pour it—and I have a feeling my opinion is not about to change. Erax, however, drinks the wine and then orders several more refills. His wine glass is soon replaced with a large goblet. All the while, he holds my hand and pays thanks to those in his court offering their blessings and gifts. The latter is placed on a long table at the other side of the room, and it's not long before the entire surface is covered in gifts.

After an hour of this, I squirm in my chair, my bones growing tired and achy. Erax snaps his fingers, and a servant holds out a glass filled with red wine.

"Here, drink it." He nudges the glass towards me. "It makes sitting here for long periods more bearable."

I stare at the wine glass. The colour reminds me of the blood he pressed to my lips before he kissed me.

"No, thank you."

Erax raises his eyebrows in mock surprise. "Does my wife not trust her own husband?"

I glare at him, painfully aware of the smile threatening my lips. "Your wife doesn't trust you as far as she can throw you." I remove my hand from his. The absence of his warmth is instantly noticeable. "Besides, I'm allergic."

"Mm. Convincing."

Before I can claim my hand back, Erax grabs hold of me again. In one quick stride, he pulls me onto his lap, and his free hand falls upon my waist. I let out a surprised squeal as our faces are brought dangerously close, mere inches apart. A slight flush colours his smooth cheeks as he looks down at me. Even now, he still has to tilt his head. My own cheeks flush as I hold his stare.

Then, when I think I can't possibly turn redder, he pulls me in for a kiss.

My entire body flares as it's pressed against him, and my lips immediately part, as though they know exactly what this captor wants of me: to surrender, to obey. His tongue slides between them, taking mine prisoner, and a strange, bitter taste trickles to the back of my throat. It's not unpleasant.

It's strong, like his scent, which is invading my very lungs.

When Erax pulls away, there's a grin on his lips. "Still allergic?"

"Y-yes," I lie again, "and it still tastes foul."

I try to climb off his lap, but he tightens his hold on me. I search his gaze questioningly. There's a dark glint in them that makes me stay quiet for a moment.

"You'll sit here, wife, until you go into anaphylactic shock."

"I—" I cut myself off. How can I get out of this now? I don't want to sit on his lap, and in front of so many people. I catch a glimpse of Noble smirking at me as he passes the foot of the dais, ordering the servants to bring more wine and ale. "Fine. I hope you're prepared to bury your wife on the same day as you married her."

Erax digs his fingers into my hip, making me wince.

"I was joking," I say, not sure why I'm whispering or feeling the need to explain myself.

Erax softens his grip on me, but his eyes remain just as intense. "*Don't.*"

The warning laced around that one syllable makes me shiver.

Gods above, can he not take a joke? In a way, our marriage is nothing but the biggest joke of all, but I don't say that to him. I don't like the chances of him bending me over his knee and spanking me like a child. I instead train my attention on those feasting and dancing before us. They're a good distraction, a reprieve from the man holding me prisoner in his arms.

"Here comes my other gift to you," Erax says, his voice considerably softer.

My heart jumps. "Your gifts are beginning to frighten me, Erax."

He laughs, and I hate how the sound makes me want to laugh with him. "I think you'll like this one."

I turn back to the crowd. My eyes seem to be playing tricks on me, because for a moment, I think I see my uncle working his way towards us. And then he stops by the bottom of the dais, removes his hat, and bows.

"Uncle?!"

I practically choke the word out as I push Erax away and climb off his lap.

"Pardon my tardiness, Your Royal Highnesses, but there was a delay on the road. Fortunately, one of your dragon riders assisted me, though I must say I'm not as fond of flying as I thought I'd be in my youth. I damn near fell off and succumbed to death." He raises his head, his eyes flickering between us before settling on me, and a sad smile twists his rugged lips. "Maelena. How the sun itself fails to rival your beauty on this day."

Tears prick my eyes and, customs be damned, I climb off the dais and leap into my uncle's arms. He catches me, albeit a little surprised, and I'm very aware of everyone watching us, but I don't care. Even if my uncle played a part in all this, I've missed him too much, and how I have longed to hug him. He's the familiar face I've been searching for. One of them, at least.

His arms enfold me in a familiar, much needed embrace as I glance at Erax from the corner of my eye. Now this gift... this gift I could get used to. He clears his throat, and my uncle lets me go. Straightening, he bows again to the king, keeping one arm around my back to grasp my shoulder.

"Your Majesty, I am honoured to be celebrating this day with you. To see my niece in such spirits..." His eyes cloud with tears and his throat jerks. "You have given this old warrior a reason to smile again."

"I hope not too old," Erax replies, his hands draped over the armrests. "I was told you were the best warrior in the old kingdom and that you know these lands better than any mortal."

"I know them like the back of my hand, Your Majesty."

"Then later you and I will discuss having you join my guard. They could do with learning some new tricks, and you are no longer of use to the convent."

Not far off to the side, Noble scoffs and mutters something under his breath. I don't think he appreciated the comment about the king's guard learning new tricks. Erax doesn't take his eyes off my uncle, who hasn't looked so happy in a very long time.

"I would be honoured, my king."

Erax makes an affirmative gesture with his hand. "Consider it done. We must talk later. Tomorrow, perhaps."

My uncle bows. "As you wish..." He trails off, and I watch the muscles along his jaw flutter. "If I could be so bold as to beseech more of your kindness, my king, and have a moment alone with my niece."

Erax regards my uncle for several moments. "Since we are kin now, I don't see why not. Noble—" He gestures to him. "Watch over them while I'm gone." Then, turning to me, he adds, "Don't get any funny ideas. I'll just be over there."

He casts a look across the room.

I nod at him and bite my lip. I have so much to discuss with my uncle, but most of all, I want to know if he knows about Lochlan. I need to know if he's safe and if he ever made it to that place where my mother was born.

"I see our king has managed to tame you," my uncle says to me, "and without noticeable injuries, which is a feat I thought no mortal capable of."

Okay. So, I no longer want to hug my uncle. I want to punch him. I forgot how annoying he could be with his teasing. Erax narrows his eyes at him. Oh. Right. He doesn't really understand the concept of a proper joke. Thankfully, with a quick glance at me, he returns my uncle's nod somewhat curtly before stepping off the dais and making his way to the banquet table. He is immediately surrounded by his people. Noble leans against the side of his vacant throne, his arms folded and his eyes locked on me. Does that grin ever leave his face?

I turn to my uncle. "You must tell me everything!"

He chuckles, the sound tapering into a cough. That's new. "Always eager, aren't you, my little maeflower?" He smiles at me fondly as he leads us to a quiet corner of the room. Noble follows us with his gaze. "There is not much to say. The convent is no more; the king had it burned down not long after you departed. We lost many lives that night, including our possessions. Barely anyone survived. Nasty business. I still don't know why he did it, but then, he is the king."

My heart sinks. I don't have the heart to tell him why Erax did what he did. Or rather, who for. I also don't have the heart to tell him what Sister Gabriella put me through all those years. It would destroy him.

"I was lucky to make it out alive," he continues, reaching for one of the small cakes on the dessert table. "If the boy Lochlan hadn't come back when he did, I'd be rotting in the ground with the others."

Instead of sinking, my heart leaps inside my chest, almost into the back of my throat. Lochlan... went *back*? Why? I told him to keep going and leave without me. I promised I'd meet him and that, when I did, we'd both be free again.

"How is..." I swallow the lump building in my throat, trying to appear calm. "Lochlan? Is he well?"

My uncle side-eyes me, and there's a knowing glint in his eye that makes me look away. "The boy is fit and well, but no less stupid, if you want my honest opinion. Insisted on coming here with me today. It was his fault we ended up lost and stranded and damn near became dragon lunch." My uncle licks the cream off his fingers and reaches for another. "Did you know that he has family here? An estranged brother. That gentleman over there, if you could believe it."

I follow my uncle's gaze, my heart pounding. For a moment, it stops beating when my eyes land on Noble. He's still watching us. He unfolds one arm to give me a wave, which my uncle returns. Gods above... The resemblance between Noble and Lochlan seems to slap me in the face. How did I not see it until now when it was pointed out to me?

"Does he know? Noble, I mean, that Lochlan is here?"

"I don't think he'd be alive if he did." My uncle leans in and lowers his voice. "I think the boy came here to kill him. You get to know that look in a man's eyes, and he had it."

I can't seem to look away from Noble. Why would Lochlan want to kill anyone, let alone his own brother? In all the years I've known Lochlan, he has never once displayed violent tendencies of any kind. He wanted to make the sisters pay for what they were putting us through, mostly putting me through, but he never did it. Besides, everyone who fell victim to them wanted to make them pay for their cruelty. What could Noble have done to Lochlan to warrant his own brother's hate and wish to kill him? It just doesn't seem like the sweet Lochlan I know.

"Where is Lochlan now?" I ask.

"I sent him back when he refused to get on the dragon." He pops another dessert into his mouth. I have never seen him eat so much. In fact, I didn't even know he had a sweet tooth until now. "He told me what you planned," my uncle resumes, drawing my attention away from the sweet pastry and back to him. "The escape. The boat. The servant girl who was killed trying to help you."

I don't look away, even at the mention of the girl who helped us being killed. Did Sister Gabriella do that? I try not to imagine the horrific way she would have made the innocent girl suffer.

"Uncle, where is Lochlan?" I press him again.

He lowers the pastry that was about to be inserted into his mouth, and his eyes harden, reminding me of the uncle who would scold me for *always making your life so damn difficult, Maelena*. The same eyes that used to look at me like I was his whole world, before the convent ripped him of that. That's what Sister Gabriella and her followers did: they ripped you of every little joy until there was nothing left. And yet, on the rare occasions that my uncle and I were alone, I saw glimmers of the old uncle, the one who used to tell me silly stories and make me laugh until my belly ached. Now my stomach only clenches as he grabs my arm and pushes me to the nearest window, his features veiled in anger.

"It is time you grow up and start facing reality, Maelena," he shouts in a whisper. "You are no longer a child but a woman. You are a wife now. A *queen*. You must start acting like one if we're to get out of this mess alive!" His enraged features soften a little, and so does his voice as he takes a deep breath and counts back from five. It's a technique he taught me to do when I was little as a way to calm myself.

"Maelena," he says after a moment. "You must understand that your duty is no longer to honour what's inside there"—he touches my heart, then nods over to the window—"but to honour what's outside there. Go on and look. Look at how our people are celebrating your union. Look at their merriment. Do you see them?"

Despite wanting to pull away from him, I follow his gaze to the window, where thousands of people are celebrating beyond the palace walls. Even some of the guards appear to be joining in on the songs at their stations.

"Don't you see, my child? For the first time in decades, our kingdom can rest because for once there is peace among us now. Take it from this old warrior—peace is far more precious than all the gold in the world. And as queen, it is your duty to help protect that peace." He touches my cheek gently, wiping away a tear I didn't know had fallen there. "Don't throw it all away for the heart of a boy who'd rather burn that peace to the ground. I raised you to be wiser than that, Maelena. This boy—"

"Lochlan," I cut in, as tears race down my cheeks, "his name is Lochlan, and maybe... maybe there's still a chance... I could be free again."

That we could be free.

My uncle wipes my face with his sleeve. "As I see it, a queen is never free when the weight of her crown carries the fate of her people. Perhaps if you stopped fighting your king and let the past be the past and fulfilled your royal duty, then your crown might not be so heavy."

What is he saying? Crown. Cage. They both mean the same to me now.

And royal duty? He means cementing my bond to Erax in a physical way I've never done with anyone before.

I turn around and glance around the room. My gaze instantly lands on Erax, as if called by him. I have spent most of my life crownless because of this man, who is now making his way towards me. His cruelty that awful day left me with a burden so heavy I have thought of nothing but my revenge, and

Lochlan promised to help me get it. How can I just let that all go? How can I forgive Erax and leave what he did to me in the past when it was he who so drastically altered my future?

This was never supposed to be my life, and I was never, *ever* supposed to feel happy about it. Yet when Erax kissed me inside the cathedral, it was like he had stolen something from me, because that was the happiest I've ever felt.

It turns out the king is more than just a beautiful liar.

He's a beautiful thief too.

CHAPTER ELEVEN

ERAX

I'll kill him.

I don't give a fuck if he's her uncle.

Whatever he said to make my wife cry —on the day of our wedding, no less—I'll fucking kill him for it.

I step out from the entourage of advisors and make my way across the hall. My gut clenches at the sight of my wife hugging another man, even if he is considered her family. She's crying in his arms, and he's running a hand through her hair and patting her back in comfort. I clench my own hands into fists and clasp them behind my back to keep from raising them.

You need to take a deep fucking breath, Erax.

She's your wife, and that's her uncle. Breathe, damn it!

As I reach the halfway point, Noble stands in my way. The grin on his face makes me want to punch him more violently than it usually does. I need to cool it with alcohol. I've never handled it as well as some men. Fuck, Noble has been able to drink me under the table multiple times. But ever since this princess entered my life, a drink of something heavy seems to be the only thing capable of distracting me from her. It's not the alcohol that poisons my veins—it's her.

"Move," I growl.

Noble remains blocking the way. "I have much to tell you, my king."

"Not now."

"Erax—"

"Just leave me fucking be!"

"I would if you didn't look like you were about to kill a man." The idiot follows my line of sight, and his eyebrows lift. "Ah... Wait, is that not her uncle?" When I continue glaring at him, he says, "Fuck, Goldeye. The princess has really done a number on you."

"Queen," I counter, "and you have exactly

225

five seconds to move before I cut out that useless tongue of yours and feed it to the castle cats."

He moves aside quickly, and it's then I notice Maelena has gone. Her uncle stands by the buffet, indulging himself. Time for some family bonding, I think.

I ignore Noble's remarks and march over to the uncle.

"My king." He bows, and that familiar smile creeps over his face again.

The false one I can spot a mile off.

It's a smile I have seen members of my grandfather's court give when I was a child and caught them scheming against him. The kind of tight smile that barely even reaches one's eyes. I never said anything or alerted my grandfather when I did catch people scheming against him. I stayed in the shadows and watched them fulfil their duties to the crown with that smile on their faces, all whilst plotting his demise so I could take his seat after my father died in battle when I was a child. They didn't want another king like my grandfather.

Some days I'm not sure if their efforts

paid off and if I'm any better than him. But then I remind myself that no one has tried to kill me yet, so that's got to count for something. My wife seems to be their target right now, according to my spies, which is why I have tripled my guard since bringing her here. I return her uncle's smile just as tightly.

"Perhaps it was the light, but did I just witness you making my wife cry on our wedding day?"

"Forgive me, my king. It appears Maelena still looks to the past when she should be embracing the future, and I simply reminded her of that."

I nod, tightening my hands behind my back. I can't blame her for looking back at her old life. I took it from her and, given the chance, I'd do it again. No amount of bodies I pile at her feet will remedy that.

"It also appears that the absence of her friend opened an old wound," he continues, snapping my interest back to him. "I had the boy escort me from our settlement. Not entirely useless, but terrified of dragons. The queen was dismayed when he did not attend the feast to congratulate her."

The muscles in my throat tighten. I know exactly who the fuck he is referring to. The male who tried to help her escape. I recall little about him other than the way he had looked at Maelena, and the way she tried to protect him. I knew he was hidden by the crates all along, but I let her believe otherwise. I had Noble drag his ass back to the convent where, I believe, he was punished. I had wanted to kill him for nearly taking my future wife away from me.

"What is this *boy's* name?" I ask, enjoying demeaning him.

No one takes my wife from me—especially not that worthless piece of shit.

"Lochlan. I hired him when... well, when things were different. Afterwards, you then instructed him to assist me and the sisters at the convent as a means of protection."

I sneer at that. "I did not think stealing qualified as protecting, or has the meaning of the word changed?"

"Of course not, Your Majesty. I made sure the boy was suitably punished for daring to steal the king's property."

Hearing someone else regard my wife as

property pisses me off. There is also something about this male that doesn't sit right.

I nod instead, my focus straying to the doors she left through. The clock mounted on the wall beside them, next to the white stag head chimes eight o'clock. Noble had placed a bet with me that my wife would run away from the feast no later than ten o'clock so she could barricade her room door. I said eight, and it appears I was right. Somehow that doesn't make me feel any fucking better.

She'll probably have a whole firing squad waiting for me tonight, but it won't stop me fulfilling my duty. I'd be lying if I said I haven't been thinking about consummating our bond and how soft her naked body would feel under my own. And try as my new wife might, she can't stop herself from thinking about it too. I could practically smell her need radiating from her when I kissed her. Fuck, I almost threw her off my lap and carried her to our room hours ago. It's been fucking torture waiting. But now the torture ends.

"Make sure the boy never steps foot in this palace," I tell him, "or I'll have his head."

I don't wait for his reply. Only a fool would disobey my order.

I head to the door, grabbing a bottle of wine from a servant.

"Would you like a glass, Your Majesty?"

"I'd like another bottle."

Another bottle is quickly given, and I leave the hall without so much as a backwards glance. I drink most of the first on my way up the endless number of staircases. Why the fuck did my grandfather build so many of them? When I enter the courtyard, the cold breeze hits, and the world around me spins. *Shit!*

I steady myself against a statue, the god of the sun. He looks down at me, *sneers* down at me, and I throw the empty wine bottle against him. I've always hated this statue. It was my grandfather's favourite. I lift my robes and take my cock out, pissing against the stone.

"Nothing to see here, Burning God," I say to the sky. "I'm just saying hello to the bastard who raised me."

When I'm done, I wash my hands in a nearby fountain—*fuck it*—and open the second bottle of wine. It's half finished by the time I'm standing outside my wife's room. I twist the handle, surprised to find it unlocked. Even more surprising are the lack of guards outside the room and the fact that my wife isn't fucking inside.

"Where is she?" I swing around and then out into the hall. "Where's my wife?"

Noble, ever the watchful one, always in my fucking shadow, appears at the end of the corridor.

"You had her sent to the honeymoon chamber, remember?"

I don't, but I shrug all the same. In truth, I've been preparing for her running away since day one. Noble follows me to where I had the bridal suite prepared. It's the biggest chamber in the palace, and I had hoped we would share it. However, the fact my wife probably sees it as nothing more than another cell makes me want to heave. Damn it, I didn't want any of this either. I didn't want to be king, and I sure as fuck didn't want to destroy her whole kingdom that day. It was either her kingdom or mine, and I'd make the same choice again if I had to. My hands were tied. They were fucking tied, Maelena!

"I'll stand guard outside," Noble says once we reach the room.

"Sure, you will." I laugh as I take a final drink of the wine and wipe my mouth with the back of my sleeve. "My wife's body is for my eyes only, and so are her screams."

I already made sure my court would not be present for the consummation. Noble is deluded if he thinks I'll make an exception for him. The fucking pervert. He can take the sheets for all I care and prove that my wife and I fulfilled our royal duties. Until sunrise, however, my wife's moans will be for my ears only.

I open the door and close it quietly behind me, locking it. The chamber's fire has been put out, and all the candles have been snuffed apart from one on the bedside table. Its amber glow bleeds over my wife already asleep in the four-poster bed, her body surrounded by piles of useless silk pillows.

"Mist?"

A smile threatens my lips as she continues to feign sleep. I take a step towards her, unbuttoning my tunic and sliding it over my head, then reach for my belt. If my wife thinks pretending to sleep will get her out of consummating our marriage, she doesn't know her husband at all.

CHAPTER TWELVE

I hear him shouting for me in the corridors. Whether by instinct or insanity, I keep my knife hidden under my pillow, my fingers wrapped around the gilded handle.

The door opens and my heart leaps into my throat. My husband's breathing is ragged and his footsteps heavy as he stumbles into the wedding chamber.

Several moments pass before he moves or speaks. All the while, I think I'm about to choke on my own heart as it thrashes in my throat.

"Mist?"

I keep my eyes closed despite my instincts telling me to open them. *Never turn your back on a predator.* Which is what I'm doing right now. However, the silence that follows is far more terrifying than any sarcastic remark he could make. He knows that I'm pretending to sleep. I can just sense that he knows, and he's probably looking down at me with a smirk on his face.

I grip my knife tighter.

I know what is expected of me on the wedding night and, as king, Erax too. The consummation is something neither of us can avoid. But that doesn't mean I can't fight it.

Erax moves over to the side of the bed. Through the barest slit of my eyes, I can see he's half naked and that his trousers are loose, his belt hanging open at his hips. Again, he doesn't move or speak. He doesn't even touch me. He just watches me, as if debating with himself. Every inch of my body flares under his close scrutiny. This is it. This is the moment I've dreaded more than any other.

In my fear, I clench my eyes, completely forgetting I'm pretending to be asleep. Erax takes a step, and I hold my breath, waiting for the moment he throws himself on me. The moment doesn't come. Much to my own surprise, and instant relief, he moves away and collapses none too quietly on the chaise lounge near the foot of the bed.

I let several minutes pass before braving a glance at him to confirm. His tall, muscular body practically swallows up the chaise. His arms and legs hang over the sides as the moonlight bleeds over him from the balcony doors. His breathing is loud, almost like he's fallen asleep. I press up onto an elbow to get a better look at him. Snoring lightly, his head rests to the side, which causes dark, dishevelled hair to fall over his eyes. He is sleeping.

A surprised laugh quietly leaves me as I stare at him. I don't know what's worse, the fact he didn't wake me up or the fact my husband has fallen asleep on our wedding night, as if I'm not worth the air he breathes, let alone consummating our marriage. Why am I even mad about that?

I've dreaded this moment—*dreaded it*—since I was a young girl. I should feel relieved instead of rejected. And that hurts. It really, really hurts. Because to be rejected by someone you love is one thing. But to be rejected by your enemy? That's another thing altogether, and something about it just hits harder. It stings.

I throw my legs over the side of the bed. Removing my knife from under the pillow, I tiptoe over to him. My bare feet are nearly silent as they pad against the dark wooden floor towards my target. As I hang over his sleeping body, the knife clenched in my hand, the sharpened blade gleaming in the moonlight, I know there is a part of me that doesn't want to kill him. But this man—this beautiful thief and monster—is the reason for so much of my suffering. He's the reason I will never be free. I will always be bound to him and to a kingdom I wanted no part of.

So long as this man is alive, our destinies will forever be entwined, and it's the other part of me, the part that wants him dead, that knows that would never have happened had he not rained fire upon my world that day.

"Mmm," Erax mutters in his sleep, turning his head to face my own. His eyes remain closed. "Mmm... Mist."

That stupid part of me, the part that

doesn't want to kill him, it lowers my arm. He's... dreaming about me?

I hesitate for an instant, only an instant, when his dark lashes suddenly lift, and those piercing eyes cut right through me. In another instant, Erax grabs both of my wrists and pulls me down on top of him, our bodies flush to each other. My grip slides on the knife, but I manage to keep a hold of it, angled awkwardly over our heads.

"Second time lucky, darling?"

His breath sweeps over my cheeks, his scent invading my senses.

"This time I won't miss," I snap. "I'll make sure it works."

He sighs. "When will you learn," he says, adjusting his hips, forcing me to slide between his legs, "that you can't kill a dragon rider unless you kill their dragon. We are immortal. I'll never die and that's good because I want to haunt you forever. I'll snap that pretty neck of yours before you ever get the chance."

He squeezes his thighs and I let out a gasp as the muscles in his legs crush me. Not only that, but his member presses against me, and he's hard. The realisation on my face twists into horror.

Erax chuckles. "Alright. I'll give you another shot under one condition."

I glare at him, trying to pull my hand down to hold the knife at his throat. I can't move.

I hiss at him, "What condition?"

"You kiss me," he replies coolly, his eyes intent on me, "and I mean really fucking kiss me, wife, like you just can't breathe without me. Think you can do that?"

The gleam in his eyes makes me shiver. He can't be serious. He's giving me the chance to kill him again if I kiss him like I mean to? He must still be drunk, because he might as well be asking me to pluck the moon from the sky itself. I can't give him a kiss like that. It means I will have given in and surrendered to him. And yet, I let his hands pull me down, forcing our lips to meet, and I know at that moment, I'm a goner. He's won. He's completely won.

My knife clatters to the floor as our kiss deepens. He wraps an arm around my waist and holds my throat with his other hand, blocking out any chances of escape. Horrifyingly, I no longer seek a way out. I let my body take over, and I practically melt in his arms, surrendering myself to him not just physically but mentally too. And I hate myself for it.

I hate *him* for making me this way.

I drag my nails down his bare chest, clawing at his flesh in resentment, and bite his upper lip until his blood dances over my tongue. He groans into my mouth as he assails me with his own tongue, drawing unbidden moans from the depths of my throat. Gods above, I hate him.

I've hated Erax with every ounce of my being since day one.

But I don't kiss him like I hate him. I kiss Erax like he's the air to my lungs, without which I would die. I kiss him just like he told me to. And he kisses me back just as eagerly, except there's something different about it.

Something dark, and hungry.

I dig my fingers into his shoulders as he lifts my hips and settles me over his groin. His erection presses against me, and I let out a moan against his lips. Erax devours it, covering my mouth with his own, and I can feel him grower bigger against me. Hungrier. My body shivers and tears leak from the corner of my eyes. I close them and dig my nails deeper into his skin.

"Look at me," Erax whispers.

I shake my head. I'm too afraid to look at him. Afraid I'll give in.

He rests his forehead against mine, his warm breath fanning my flushed cheeks. "As your king, I am commanding my beautiful, stubborn wife to look at me."

I open my eyes, not because he told me to, but because my heart begs me to. Erax searches my gaze and slowly tucks a strand of my hair behind my ear. His hand lingers on my cheek, the tip of his thumb catching a tear.

"What do you want from me, Mist?"

"I want to keep hating you," I breathe out, my words trembling.

For a moment, he says nothing. He caresses me and looks intensely into my eyes, flicking between them. It's like he's searching for something only I can give him. I hold my breath, and the fleeting ray of moonlight that catches his eyes makes them shimmer like emerald and gold glass. They are so beautiful.

"Then hate me," he says, "just don't fucking run from me again, or I'll be the one holding a knife to *your* throat. Got it?"

He kisses me again, his touch deep and possessive. His words should frighten me; the severity behind them is clear. Yet they only awaken a part of me I had no awareness of until this moment. It's like a deep, primal need that now urges me to surrender my body to him and to explore his, staking my claim over it. It's this need that frightens me most of all. It frightens me more than anything.

I let the fear pull me away from him. However, Erax is quick to grab hold of my hair, and he yanks me down with a quick, painful tug.

"No," he warns.

"Erax..." His name is breathless on my lips, a plea. "Let me go."

He tightens his grip on my hair. "I'm not letting go of my queen for anyone."

"Not even for the gods?" I gasp as he tugs again, snapping my head back.

"Especially not for them. *It's you for me.*"

Then he pulls me back down again and reunites our lips in a deep, passionate kiss that literally takes my breath away. It's like he's trying to steal the air out of my very lungs. He keeps his fingers twisted through my hair and his other hand on my hips as he grinds me against him. His tongue spears my mouth, devouring me, and I stop fighting him. I stop running away. In that instance, I no longer want to do either of those things.

I just want to feel, to touch and taste his body.

Claim him, that primal side of me whispers. *Claim him like he wants to claim you.*

Try as I might, I can no longer deny this bond between us. It's growing stronger every time our lips meet. Every time he looks at me with that hunger in his eyes. Every time he touches me and calls me *his*. I can't deny our bond, and as he anchors my legs to his waist and lifts me over to the bed, I finally realise that deep down, I don't want to. This is a battle I can longer fight.

A mix between a sob and a moan escapes me as he rests me on a velvet ottoman by the front of the bed. Without taking his eyes off me, he lowers himself to his knees, his eyes coming level with my own. His hands find purchase on my ankles. Slowly he glides his palms up my legs, and my silk green nightgown slides over them. Oh, gods above! My cheeks flush as I recall the ridiculous outfit I'm wearing.

Even though I didn't have much of a choice in the matter, it's still embarrassing to be wearing something so revealing. This stupid nightgown was the only piece of clothing the servants brought with them. Well, that and the very tight and very fancy white lace undergarments I'm wearing underneath. I only agreed to them because I figured attempting to kill my new husband naked wasn't my brightest plan of attack.

Erax reaches for the nightgown's many thin lace straps. They cut across each other on the bodice, starting just below the plunging neckline. They're not tight like a corset but still snug enough to look like one, and it felt like forever until the servants were done fastening them. Mostly because the same lace straps run down my arms as well as my chest and back. With a quick glance down at myself, I quickly realise that the most embarrassing factor of all isn't the gown itself.

No. Of course there had to be something more embarrassing.

It's that the white undergarments underneath can be seen even through the nightgown.

Erax doesn't take his eyes off me. He continues to unfasten the laces on my torso and then my back. He only loosens the ones on my arms before he slides the nightgown down my torso, the material puddling at my waist.

I raise my hips, allowing Erax to slide the nightgown off me. He tosses it to the side, and a light chill caresses me as he trails his eyes over my body before he removes my undergarments too. First the bralette, then the underwear, followed by the see-through stockings, which he unrolls slowly off my legs one after the other. His throat jerks and his pupils are dilated when he finally takes me in, now lying naked before him, totally exposed and vulnerable.

"Fuck."

The word startles me. I hug my arms close to my chest. "Fuck?"

"Fuck," Erax repeats, pulling my hands away. "As in, fuck, this beautiful goddess is my wife. Fuck, only I get to see her like this. Fuck, I'll kill any god or mortal who touches or sees my wife's naked body. And fuck, I'm about to be inside her. That's what I mean by fuck."

I don't pull away or try to cover myself again. I scarcely even breathe as he runs his hands up my body, beginning at my knees. The way he looks at every inch of my skin makes me feel more alive than I have ever felt before. Like my body was meant to be his. It responds like it does. Is it like this for everyone? Does it always feel this good when you're touched? He trails the tips of his fingers up my thighs and over my stomach. Goosebumps raise the hairs on my skin everywhere he touches. It's like he's setting every scar on fire, burning them with his touch.

His hand cups my breast and gently he caresses me. I don't know why I do it, but I arch my back and push myself against him. My nipple rubbing his palm sends a jolt of pleasure circulating through me. His murmur is like poison sweeping throughout my body and taking everything. "So responsive for me." I let out a quiet moan as my most sensitive area grows hot and tingles between my thighs. I've never done this before, and I don't know right from wrong, but this feels good, and I don't want him to stop.

Erax doesn't stop. He stretches up until his mouth claims my other breast, and then he flicks his tongue over my pebbled nipple.

Fuck was right. Why does this already feel so good?

Back and forth he flicks his tongue before taking my nipple between his teeth. He bites down and I let out a surprised gasp, followed by a moan as he softly kisses me. Then his tongue works its way down my body. He trails his lips over my stomach down to my inner thighs. He bites me there as he lifts my ankle and rests it over his shoulder. He does the same with my other leg, draping it over his shoulder.

"Lie back," he whispers against my thigh. "I want to taste you."

I do as he says, and he parts me that bit wider.

The moment his tongue finds its place between my legs, I reach for his hair, grabbing hold of him as though I'm about to fall. His breath tickles me as his chuckles increase my pleasure. I bite my lower lip to keep from gasping out again and focus on letting that pressure grow until it spreads over my body in a wave. I've never felt anything like it. I've had orgasms before, by myself, but they weren't like this. It's more intense, more everything, with Erax.

The long sweeps of his tongue, the gentle breaths and relentless swirling, are unlike anything I have experienced. It's unlike anything I could have imagined. Erax laps at me as if I'm honey, the very nectar to his being. His fingers move from my inner thigh to caress my folds. He spreads me out, the tip of his tongue searching for that little bud. I feel him moan against me when he finds it, and the sound is beyond erotic.

I want to hear it again.

I twist my hips and try to angle them to give him better access. Or rather, make it easier for him. But Erax presses a hand to my stomach and firmly pushes me down, pinning me to the bed. His eyes flash up to me in warning.

"Stay, or I will tie you to this bed."

I follow his glance to where leather restraints hang from the bottom of the bedposts, some of them clearly visible. How did I miss those?

"You came—*aah!*—prepared."

I gasp as he flicks his tongue over me again, right over my sweet spot.

Erax grins up at me. "Of course I did. I know my wife better than anyone. Better than you." He glides his tongue over the length of my core. "Just like I know all this delicious wetness is for me." He groans as he breathes me in. "Now this is the feast I've been waiting for."

Erax doesn't tease me with his tongue. He devours me with it.

He uses the tip to coax out moan after moan until my legs are trembling underneath him. A warm sensation gathers inside me, and I dig my nails into his scalp, but then he just pulls away, and that beautiful, warm feeling vanishes.

A wicked grin taunts his lips when he looks up at me. "Not yet, Mist. The next one I want something different."

He reaches for my hand and removes it from his hair. Something tells me he meant for that to happen—for my pleasure to build and then stop. *Tyrant.* He lifts my hips, wrapping my legs around his waist, and with another wicked grin, throws me back onto the bed. He then climbs onto me, draping his powerful body over mine, and places his hands at either side of my face.

I look up into his eyes, at my reflection staring right back, completely exposed and vulnerable to this man before me. He's worse than a tyrant—he's a cold-blooded conqueror. For a moment, flashes of that familiar hatred rise to my surface. As if sensing it, Erax pins my hands above my head.

"I just want to touch you."

"Sure you do." He smirks down at me. "Claw my eyes out, more like."

I curse under my breath, and he laughs.

Then he kisses me, and at first, I wince from my taste on his lips. Until that wince turns into a moan when I feel him press against me. He's so hard, and so big. He slides his cock between my legs and rubs against me, almost like he's marking me with his scent. I should find it odd, but for some reason, it makes me open my legs wider to welcome him in. He's marking me because he's about to claim me.

"What's wrong?" I ask when he suddenly stops.

"Nothing. I'm just looking at you."

My cheeks flame and I turn my head to the side, feeling strangely shy.

"Don't," Erax orders, the command clear in his voice. "I want my wife to look at me when I enter her for the first time."

I take a deep breath and blink back up at him. He moves towards me and glides the tip of his member against my opening. His eyes never leave mine as he enters me. Slowly he pushes inside, inch by inch, and I bite my lips to keep from crying out. It hurts, it stings, but Erax's eyes hold me in their grasp, forcing me to focus only on him. He presses his forehead to mine as he eases further in.

I dig my nails into his hand, groaning with him once he's fully inside me. For a moment, he stays like that, our bodies entwined, as if he's savouring the moment. I savour it too. My hate for him no longer burns with just hatred, but desire too. A yearning so fierce that it sears my very soul.

Tears leak from the corner of my eyes. He watches them fall as he moves his hips, and I feel myself stretching around him. Then he leans down and licks them from my cheek. He caresses the side of my face with his hands, freeing mine to fall upon his back. I dig my fingers into his skin there, half of me wanting to rip the flesh from his bones, and the other half—the half that terrifies me most of all—wants to caress him back. To just see what it would feel like to open myself up to him.

Who am I kidding? I opened myself to Erax the moment he kissed me.

He groans as I claw at him. His hand wraps around my neck and squeezes in warning. I hold his gaze and let him look me in the eye just like he wanted. His grip tightens and he presses his fingers into my throat as he moves his hips with not so gentle thrusts. His movements are no longer gentle or slow but fast and deep, each one hitting off a strange spot inside me that makes me curl my toes.

I close my eyes, shocked by the sensation and frightened by the urge I have to kiss the man causing it. Erax squeezes my throat harder, and stars spread across my vision.

"Open them!"

I obey his command with a moan. How can Erax make me moan like this while practically choking me? How can my body even enjoy this? But my body is more than enjoying it, because the stars that dance across my vision work their way into my hands and toes, and I dig them into whatever surface I can as I scream out.

"*Erax!*"

The sensation building in me is just too great. Too strong. It makes me want to scream and cry at the same time. My eyes close again from instinct as this orgasm hits harder than the last and simply blinds me with sheer pleasure.

"Look at me!" Erax moves faster, his hand never leaving my throat. "Stop fighting me, Maelena, and look at me."

Breathlessly, I look up at him glaring down at me. The tips of his cheeks are flushed, his breathing has turned heavy, and his hair is dishevelled, falling into his eyes. Eyes that are so terrifying and mesmerising at the same time. Eyes that take my breath away. Eyes that tear me apart and make me want to submit to him.

"Just stop fighting me," Erax repeats, his voice bordering on a plea.

I'm not fighting you.

I want to scream the words at him, but I can only moan again as his thrusts deepen, lifting me off the bed. I cling to his shoulders, finding his lips with my own. Erax pauses, as if shocked by the kiss. Somewhere in the coherent part of my mind, it takes me by surprise too, but I don't pull away. I kiss Erax like he really is the air to my lungs, my reason for breathing.

"Maelena…" He moans out my name like it's a prayer. "My wife… *Fuck*!"

He stills inside me, releasing with a deep, shuddering groan that makes me clench around him. Minutes pass while the two of us lie sprawled on the bed, utterly spent, and I realise with beautiful, devastating conviction that Erax has more than won the battle between us.

He's completely conquered me.

CHAPTER THIRTEEN

"Maelena, wake up."

"No!" I fight the arms trying to pull me awake as I stare down at my parents' burned faces. Ash swirls in the air around me, falling to a black, scorched earth engulfed in flames. "NO!"

An enormous shadow stretches over me, devouring the sunlight.

I know this dream. I have dreamt it a thousand times over; it always starts and ends with fire. But this time, the dream is different. When I fall to the ground, I'm not burned alive by the dragon circling the clouds above. This time, my hands fall into an icy sea of roses, and they're pulling me under, dragging my whole body in until I'm almost frozen in place. I use what strength I have to claw my way through them, grasping petal after petal, my hands scratched and bleeding from the shards, but nothing brings me back to the surface. I'm drowning.

"*Maelena*!"

I open my eyes with a quick breath. Erax hangs over me, his features etched with worry. Tears sting my eyes, but for some reason, I can't hold them back anymore.

"Why did you do it?" I ask, my voice barely audible even to my ears.

Erax pauses for a moment before he moves back. "Do what?"

My heart clenches with an abrupt pain that stabs me in the chest.

"Kill my parents." I turn my head to look at him, my tears sliding into the silk pillow. "Why did you kill them?"

For a long moment, Erax is silent. He holds my stare and there is a glow in his eyes from the dying firelight that reminds me of the flames from that very night. He drags a hand through his hair and shakes his head. Then, with a glance at me, he eases out of the bed. I hold the coverlet to my chest and watch him pull on his trousers and shirt, followed by his boots. He picks up his cloak from the back of a chair and offers it to me.

"I'll show you," he says, "but I don't want to kill every guard we pass on the way." He nods to the ottoman where he... My cheeks flush as I recall him between my legs and the moans he made me cry out. "There are clothes and boots in there. Gloves too. You'll need them."

With a curious nod, I slide out of the bed with the cover still draped over me, and tiptoe to the ottoman. I somehow manage to open the lid without dropping the cover to the floor, a feat that seems to amuse my shameless spectator.

"Why do you still hide from me, Mist?" He tosses the cloak on the bed and helps keep the ottoman open for me. "It's not like I haven't seen your gorgeous body. Or licked every square inch of it. Stop hiding."

Damn him! My blush increases tenfold. I try to focus hard on pulling out several items of clothing and a pair of black boots that appear to be my size. I wish I'd thought about checking the ottoman earlier. It might have saved me from having to wear that embarrassing nightgown. I find the very item on the floor, and I stuff it inside the ottoman before closing it over. Hopefully, I won't need to wear it again anytime soon.

"Pity," Erax sighs. "I rather liked that on you, but I won't have anyone else seeing you wearing it. It's not really fitting for where we're going anyway."

I hate the way my heart jumps at the possessiveness in his tone.

"Where are we going?" I ask, pulling a pale blue tunic over my shoulders.

"Somewhere I should've taken you weeks ago."

The tunic falls low enough that I don't need to wear leggings. I tie the straps at my waist and then pull on the boots. Erax holds the cloak out for me. I turn around and let him drape it over my shoulders. His fingers brushing my neck sends a shiver through me.

"You're not going to give me another gift again, are you?" I follow him out of the room. "Your gifts really are starting to frighten me."

He laughs, and my heart does that stupid jump again. "I'm going to give you something better than a gift. The truth."

Outside of the chamber, he pulls a torch from the wall, and takes my hand in his. With a nod to his guards, bidding them to stay, he then leads the way again. The palace is eerily quiet as we walk. I remain just a step behind him, and I use the opportunity to trail my eyes over his towering body. His hair is tousled, and his skin looks like burnished gold in the firelight. His white shirt is only half tucked into his trousers, but his sleeves are rolled to the elbow, like I've seen him do a few times. And yet, as he holds the torch in his hand, the muscles in his forearm ripple and flex, and I don't know why I find that so attractive. I need to get a hold of myself.

Erax said he's going to show me the truth, and *that's* what I need to focus on.

Not his forearm. Or the way his back muscles are straining that shirt. Or his—

Dead parents, stolen kingdom, brutal captivity. Remember those things, Maelena?

We can't let a gorgeous thief make us forget them. Even if he is our husband.

Even if he is the king. Even if I can still feel where he was inside me, making me feel more alive than I ever have before.

We pass several guards on the way to the keep. I'm only certain we're headed there when we reach the familiar red door, and the distinct burning smell invades my nostrils. My pulse instantly increases. Okay, now I'm really getting nervous. The last time I was brought down here, Erax killed people in my name. Granted, they were terrible, awful people, but I can still hear their screams lurking in the shadows around me. It's like they're echoing with my every step.

Erax squeezes my hand, almost like he's trying to offer me comfort. I squeeze him back, even though I can still hear my parents' screams too. They're fresh in my memory again thanks to the dream. Not that they ever leave. I didn't see them die or even hear them die, but my imagination makes something up. It always does.

When we emerge into the beginning of the den, the place appears to be empty. Only the sound of our boots echoing on the steps leading down fills the silence. And then a robed figure steps out of the shadows and stands on the centre of the platform—the same platform where those dead bodies had lain. *They weren't good people, and they got the ending they deserved.* I try to remind myself of that and not think about them as I climb onto the platform with Erax. He's still holding my hand.

"This is Zepheira," he says, nodding to the other person. "Grand dragonmeyer to the realm, protector of our dragons. Royal pain in the ass some days."

"And other days, grandmother to my delightful grandson."

The woman drops her hood, revealing a head of thick braided silver hair with gold clasps woven in them. They fall over her dark face when she bows, and they briefly shadow her features. "Your Majesties, it is truly an honour to see you both together." Then to Erax, she adds, "It is about time you brought your beautiful wife to meet me. I have been waiting."

Oh, Zepheira is definitely related to Erax.

She's mastered that sharp, slightly disappointed, admonishing tone perfectly.

Once she straightens, the light catches her face, and I'm finally able to get a clear look at her. Zepheira is a lot older than Erax, looks to be perhaps in her late sixties, but I don't see any resemblance between them. At least not at first glance. Her skin is darker and her bone structure sharper. I'd kill to have her high cheekbones. The only similarity I see between them is their different coloured eyes. They each have a gold one on the same side.

"You both have a gold eye," I point out, glancing up at Erax. While the woman's scar begins at the side of her nose and runs all the way over her temple, entwining with her wrinkles, Erax's starts at the inner corner of his eye and falls down his cheek to the edge of his face, stopping just below his ear. "Is it an inherited defect?"

Before Erax can answer me, his grandmother lets out a choking sound.

"You mean to say the queen *does not know*?"

Erax lets go of my hand and crosses his arms, a tic pulsing in his jaw. "The queen wasn't ready."

"Well, the queen is standing right here, and I have no idea what you're talking about."

Zepheira gives her grandson what I can only assume to be a scolding look.

"Come," the old woman says to me. She loops her arm through mine and pulls me from Erax. "Let us take a walk together. You have much to see and learn, my young queen, but tonight I have something special for you. Spectacular, really. Did you know the king comes from a long line of dragonmeyers?"

"No," I say, glancing back at Erax. "I didn't."

Erax follows us closely, although he stays several steps behind. He doesn't look happy to have brought me here. I think he's definitely reconsidering. But I want to know the truth. I want to know why Erax invaded our kingdom and killed my parents when we hadn't been at war with them. In fact, I hadn't even heard of Erax until that night.

I also didn't know that his bloodline consists of dragonmeyers. I only knew that he was the one who brought them back into existence. Prior to that, dragons simply... disappeared. One moment they were there, and the next, they were gone.

Sister Gabriella said the dragons abandoned us because of our sins and that we were resisting the will of the gods. I could never find anything to confirm that in my research though, but pointing it out got a slapped cheek in front of everyone.

"A very long line of them," Zepheira continues. "It was our ancestors who witnessed the first ever documented hatching. Nightix, Cyrsí's great-great-great-great-grandfather, was said to be the child of Nytar himself. It is why all of Cyrsí's line breathe black fire that looks like it has stars within it, and they all have gold eyes."

I know her fire well, I want to say, but I just manage to hold the words back.

"How old would that make Cyrsí?"

"Oh, that stubborn beast is still very young because she belongs to Erax. Dragons are hatched for their riders, and they begin their life with a rider or dragonmeyer of their choosing. Not all dragonmeyers are riders, but more caregivers for riderless dragons. Dragons and riders are immortal together while the dragon is alive, and dragons tend to live for hundreds of years. It is painful for a rider to lose their dragon, but they can live after... just a shell of a life." Sadness lingers in her voice. "Now her grandmother, she was old, a truly magnificent beast until she died."

"What was her name?" I ask, my curiosity ripening.

"Venra. I was her rider for almost a hundred and two years. I was there when she hatched, and I was there when she took her last breath."

There's a shift in Zepheira's tone, an almost bitter note that tinges her words.

"Venra died protecting her kin. She gave her life so that her young could live on." Then, changing the subject, she says to me, "Would you like to meet Cyrsí's sister? Her brother I wouldn't introduce you to yet, but her sister can be agreeable. They're the only triplets of their kind."

I had no idea you could get twin dragons, let alone triplets.

"I'd love to meet her."

"Splendid. Now, Fynra did lay her egg recently, but I just fed her, so she should be quite tame."

"Quite tame doesn't *quite* settle my nerves."

Zepheira laughs and pats my arm. "I like you already. Come down this way."

I let her steer me towards a huge opening in the cave wall. It leads to a tunnel that is much wider and taller than I expected it to be. Glowworms and bioluminescent flowers hang low from the ceiling. I can feel the heat pulsing around me off the walls and even through my boots on the floor. The air is thick with that burning smell, so much like Erax's scent, and it makes me a little dizzy.

I press my gloved fingers against the wall for support. Suddenly I feel Erax getting close to me. His body brushes against me as he slides around us and holds out his torch. He lifts it above his head, lighting the way. Not that we need more light. But then I realise why he's doing that. The heat from the torch causes the flowers and plants to move away.

The same vegetation covers what looks to be an exit of some kind. Erax holds his torch out to them, and the vegetation shrinks away. My breath leaves me when I take in the view of the dragons' keep that I saw last night.

From across the cavern, Cyrsí flies over to us. She lands smoothly and pulls in her wings before lowering her head to her rider. Erax presses his hand and face against her nose and closes his eyes. He whispers something to her that I don't understand, yet deep inside, I feel its meaning. Mutual respect and love for each other. A bond like no other.

"The day Cyrsí lost her grandmother, she lost her eggs too. So did her sister, and Evraas, and Shadowbane. So many eggs were lost that day. It was devastating." She looks over at Erax, and her eyes have glazed over. "You think you know grief until you see a dragon mourn her babies. There is no grief greater than that. Except, perhaps, when a rider grieves for their dragon. That I would not wish on anyone."

I follow her line of sight. Erax is stroking Cyrsí, who's grumbling softly, which I figure is the dragon equivalent to a cat purring. Except it sounds more like thunder splitting across the sky after a storm. It's still loud, but not as loud as her roars. There's a softness to it I never thought a dragon capable of.

"What happened to the eggs, if you don't mind my asking?"

Erax snaps at me, "You know what happened to them."

I stare over at him, my mouth hanging open in shock. "I don't. All I know about the dragons is that one day they were here, and the next they were gone, until you found them again."

Now he's looking at me, and if I were close enough to the edge, I'm pretty sure he'd push me off. It's been a hot minute since I've seen that hateful look on his face. But unlike the last time, the look doesn't stay. Erax quickly softens his features and turns his attention back to the beast demanding pets from him.

"Erax brought me here for the truth," I say, turning back to Zepheira. "I'm ready for it. Tell me what happened."

Zepheira opens her mouth, but then an ice-cold wind blows through the cavern, followed by a deafening roar, and suddenly her mouth clamps shut again. Then her eyes widen, and she turns hastily away, her robes billowing behind her.

"The truth can wait," she says, waving us to follow. "We must go now."

"Grandmother—"

"It is time!"

Cyrsí pulls back and Erax watches her fly away again before turning around. He's not glaring at me anymore, but he has that look in his eye again that says *mine*. How a look can make my heart beat faster and forget that we ever hated each other, I will never know. But it's beginning to really scare me.

"Time for what?"

Erax makes his way down again, and I follow carefully, mindful of my steps.

"An egg is about to hatch," he answers me. "When you're bonded to a dragon, you can sense these things. It's rare for an egg to hatch without a rider present. There are thirty-two riders in my army, but no matter how many new people we bring in, none are drawn here and feel the pull anymore."

At the bottom of the stairs, he offers me his hand to help me cross the gap.

"I guess this is what Zepheira meant by something spectacular," I say, taking his hand.

He lifts me over effortlessly, but he doesn't put me down straight away. He holds me in his arms and stares deeply into my eyes, into my very soul.

"Yeah," he whispers, "I guess this is spectacular."

My breath catches in my lungs. The way Erax said that makes me think he wasn't talking about the dragon hatching. He was talking about me. He's said absurd things to me before but nothing that makes my whole body turn weak in his arms.

"ERAX!"

Slowly he sets me down and takes my hand. He then shakes his head at his grandmother's excited, albeit insistent, shouting of his name again. I have a feeling Zepheira is the only person in the entire kingdom allowed to talk to him this way. But then, she is his grandmother, and grandmothers are a different breed entirely.

"Let's go before she bursts a lung again."

"Again?" I repeat, and Erax chuckles.

I can't help but smile as I follow him down to where the dragon eggs are kept. We pass an arena on the way where the dragon riders go to train. I can hear them training as we pass by the entrance and move down towards the rushing sound of the waterfall near the back. Erax leads me to the left of it, to a large dug-in hole.

"This is the nursery," he explains. "The most vital part of the keep."

"If the realm were alive, this would be its heart," Zepheira says, appearing behind us. She pauses beside me and takes a moment to admire the view. "Isn't it spectacular?"

The word makes me look up at Erax, who winks at me.

"There is no time to waste. We have an egg to hatch!" Zepheira cuts through us carrying a steaming basin between her hands. "Ooh, I do hope this one makes it, Erax. It has been so long since one of its kind hatched. Your father, gods be with him, was a boy when it happened."

Erax snaps his attention to her. "It's an ice dragon?"

"Yes! Her mother returned just a few weeks ago, and would you believe it? She brought her egg with her. I found her swimming in a lake she had completely frozen over." *Ummm...* "Be warned, both of you, this mother is a feisty one."

"And by feisty, do you mean—"

"Three guards, all dead." Zepheira grabs several hot stones from the furnace and drops them into the basin. They hiss and sizzle when they hit the water, creating a cloud of steam. "I did warn them not to approach her, especially when she was still settling in. She seems to only let females come near her."

Erax turns to me. "You're not going near it."

"Of course, I am." I frown and cross my arms. "In case you haven't noticed, Erax, I'm female and quite capable of listening to whatever Zepheira tells me to do."

"Believe me, I have noticed my wife is female. More than noticed, in fact." His words make me blush. *Damn him!* "And you'll listen to a crazy old dragon lady but not your husband and king?" He glares at his grandmother. "I will not endanger my wife or put her at risk with an untamed dragon."

"I might be old, but I am quite capable of protecting our queen. Or do you not recall I had you down here before you could walk? We had several untamed dragons roaming the nest back then, and you remained safe." Zepheira nods over at me. "Have faith in our queen. Her Majesty will be safe so long as she listens to me."

"I'll listen," I say, my body filling with a mixture of excitement and nerves. "As long as you just fed this dragon too."

Zepheira laughs at that, a loud booming sound. "Oh, I believe her appetite has been quite satiated, my queen."

"Maelena is fine," I tell her.

Erax stares at me as if I've grown another head. "You are unbelievable."

"Thank you." I smile and return the wink he gave me before. "You're unbelievable too."

He drags his hand through his hair and gives a surprisingly loud, frustrated groan. "Un-fucking-believable," he says, peering through his fingers at me. "I think my wife is as crazy as I am."

I smile at that. "You have no idea, Erax."

For now, the truth can wait. I'm about to witness the birth of a dragon.

CHAPTER FOURTEEN

e're standing in front of the waterfall where the dragon eggs are kept hidden on the other side. It's a secret entrance only Zepheira and the dragon riders know about. The nursery is the most important part of a nest, so even though the keep is already heavily guarded, the nursery has more guards patrolling the grounds. There's even an area where the riders can rest and train between flights. Among them are women cloaked in periwinkle robes. They nod and bow as they pass, but none of them speak.

"They're nurses," Erax explains when he catches me looking at them. "They tend the eggs when Zepheira isn't around." He turns his attention back to his grandmother. "So how did my men die?"

"How do you think?" Zepheira huffs at him. "They thought they knew better than my nurses simply because they were men. Stubborn little fools. They couldn't tell a dragon from its head to its arse." She looks over at me, her eyes narrowing quizzically. "Do you know a dragon from its head to its arse, my queen?"

"I like to think I do."

Zepheira laughs again. "Then we're all good. If the mother comes back, just do what I tell you and you won't end up like those sorry bastards." At the sight of Erax's disapproval, she quickly adds, "We are all perfectly safe, Erax. Now let's go before we miss it."

Zepheira holds out a black cane with a gleaming gold tip. She pushes the edge into the waterfall, causing the water to split and fall around her. She steps through and I follow suit before Erax can stop me. I can tell by the look on his face that he's still nervous, but he follows me through, his hair slightly wet from the water. I shake my own hair as I look around me, stopping when I take in the view. The nursery is even more incredible than I imagined. Beautiful cascading waterfalls and flowers bursting from every rock make up the nursery. I can feel the magic of this place, and the feeling only grows more intense when I see the nests and the many eggs within them.

The moment Zepheira sees the egg, she halts. "Something is wrong."

She presses her hands to the shell. Both her palms glow, radiating with strange, pulsing energy. Magic?

"What is it?" Erax asks, joining us at the table. "Not another dead one?"

"No." My heart rate increases as I watch Zepheira's palms glow brighter. "Her mother —she should be here." She lowers her ear to the egg and listens.

Meanwhile, Erax rolls his sleeves and prepares to help her. I can only watch help- lessly from the sidelines even though I'm filled with a strange instinct to touch the egg. To help.

"When an egg is about to hatch," Zepheira continues, "the mother can sense it and will do just about anything to witness the birth of her young. The only time they don't is when the egg has been abandoned. But that cannot be the reason. I just fed her before the two of you arrived. Surely…"

Her eyes widen, and both of them turn their attention to me.

"What?" I glance between them. "Surely what?"

It's Erax who replies.

"A mother dragon will abandon their egg if the foetus has bonded with someone. It's the only reason, other than death, they'll leave their young."

A deafening silence stretches between all three of us. I stare at them and then down at the egg, trying to make sense of what they're saying. But it sounds as crazy to me as if they just told me I've turned into a dragon myself.

"It's bonded to you," Erax points out.

"Quick, come here." Zepheira holds out her hand, ushering me to her.

I hurry over. She takes my hand and holds it in hers against the egg. The shell feels like ice, but the moment I touch it, it sizzles as if I've just put a hot stone onto it. Zepheira gasps and slowly withdraws her hand, leaving mine alone on top of the egg. Something within me stirs and that ache under my rib turns into a feeling I can't quite describe. It's not painful anymore. It's almost... euphoric.

"Do you feel it?" Erax's voice carries over me. I nod. "Focus on it. Let it grow."

I place my other hand on the egg, and an electric current zaps through me. I don't let go. I do what Erax instructs—I focus on the strange feeling building inside me, and I hold on to it, refusing to let it go. Something deep within urges me to pick up the egg. I lift slowly, my hands shaking, as a rush of concentrated magic surges through me.

Holding the dragon egg, it truly is stunning. Stunning beyond words really. I'm completely mesmerised by its continuous and stunning shine, surpassing the beauty of any diamond or crystal I've seen in the treasury. It's the darkest shade of blue, but each curve and line of the shell is gold and silver, glittering like stars.

Magic continues to pulsate under my fingertips, vibrating with the heartbeat of the dragon inside. Strong, longer thumps than a human heartbeat. It feels almost like a countdown. The egg's magic swirls in the surrounding air, dancing to a beat of a heart I can hear as loud as the one in my chest. Am I really about to open a dragon egg? Is this even possible?

I glance over at Erax. He only brought me here to tell me the truth. I doubt he planned for me to claim my own dragon. Will he be angry? Will he try to stop me because having a bride who hates you and becomes equally as powerful as you, it could be considered a threat to him, couldn't it? But this is the moment I have been unknowingly waiting for. It just feels right to be here, at this moment, holding this dragon egg like it's been waiting for me all my life.

Footsteps echo behind us. I know we are no longer alone here, but none of it matters as much as the egg cradled preciously between my hands. We are a bond now. An intense wave of emotions wash over me as the soft blue glow radiates down my arms, across my chest until it's around my dress too. I can't do anything but stare at it, completely in awe, as it cracks down the middle and the shell falls apart in my hands, revealing a beautiful dragon curled up in my open hands. The dragon is a deep shade of ice, with white-spotted spikes running down its back, from the tip of its nose down to its arrow-head tail. Its claws are the purest colour of water, just like its crystalline eyes.

The moment it stares up at me, yawning with its little mouth, I know we are bonded for life. A bond that is different to the one I made with Erax. A bond that is timeless and infinite. The baby dragon looks up at me, and it blinks in only the way a newborn animal can. No, not it.

She.

I know she's a girl as if she whispered so into my heart somehow. And then her name comes, rolling off my tongue like I've always known it.

"Hello, Freyren."

I forget the new arrivals until suddenly Freyren hisses at them. A dragon roars somewhere from above, echoing with more roars from other dragons that join with them. They're celebrating. I look over my shoulder, just for a second. Erax is holding his hands in the air. There is no mistaking the pride in his eyes. Erax is proud of me? My heart pounds for a new reason, and I find myself wanting to smile at him. To thank him for being proud of me when I can't remember the last time someone ever was.

"Disturbing the bond is never a line anyone should cross, but my queen does not know your ancient ways."

I know he is speaking in dragon tongue to the dragons, and I'm shocked that for once I can understand him. Freyren hisses. She wants to eat him. I gently stroke her cheek. *I can't let you eat my husband yet.*

Because if anyone is going to kill Erax, it will be me, even if the thought doesn't make me happy like it used to. Traitorous heart, this is all your fault.

"Mist, you need to go into the water right now to complete the bond and save both your lives."

Freyren snarls at him, climbing up onto my arm. His eyes widen as he gets a full look at her, and there is no mistaking the awe in his voice. "I'm no threat, ice dragon, but even you will not come between my queen and me. Now both of you, in the water, before it is too late."

My hands shake as I carry Freyren over the remains of the broken dragon egg and step into the blue shimmering water before the waterfall. The warm water itself glows where I walk, and the dragon's smoke from above almost makes me choke as I keep walking, knowing they are watching me from above. One breath of fire, one bite, and I'm gone. I can't stop shaking as I sink deeper into the water, and I only look back when I hear Erax shout.

The dragon riders, all of Erax's friends, fill the cave, but Erax holds a fist up, stopping them at his side. His eyes do not leave me. He is supporting me, even in this. I turn, looking up at the waterfall I'm coming up to, water spitting all over my body the closer I get. I don't want to soak this poor little dragon as it brushes its head under my chin from my crossed arms. I frown, looking down at the heavy falling water, right before Freyren jumps out of my arms. She dives into the water as the current pushes me through the waterfall. Heavy water blasts down on my body, and when I come out the other side, I wipe my eyes, hardly believing what I'm seeing.

There's no longer a small baby dragon, but standing in the middle of ten cluster nests of faded eggs is a fully grown, massive ice blue dragon. My dragon. Freyren. She has silver horns now, curling around her head, and a chest of blue fur, but she looks the same. Only bigger. Much bigger. She lowers her head, blowing cold air out of her mouth, and an icy breeze makes me shiver more than fear.

Freyren walks around me and settles down in the water, stretching out her magnificent, almost transparent blue wings. It's hard to look away from her, but when I do look back, all I feel is sadness at the eggs sitting out here alone. They're different from the others. None of them glow like Freyren's did, and they're not radiating with pulsing magic. It's like they're... dead. Or dying. Is this what Erax wanted to show me? Did my parents have something to do with this?

Freyren spreads her wing further, blocking the fall of the waterfall with one wing, and I see Erax talking with Noble on the other side. Both of them swiftly turn to look at me.

"You need to come out," Erax shouts.

"I know, but..." I look back at the eggs, feeling wrong about leaving them.

I can't just leave them here. The same feeling that prompted me to pick up Freyren's egg prompts me to swim back to them. I drift to the nearest clusters of eggs, and only then do I feel hot air on the back of my neck. An animalistic growl echoes in the air, and I glance up, seeing a dragon I don't know above me on a ledge, watching my every move. This one clearly feels threatened by me. There are so many dragons here, all of them hiding in the caves, their eyes always watching. I should leave, but I can't seem to bring myself away.

In the nest at my feet are twelve eggs. Two of them are still coloured, red and green, but the others are dull grey. The glowing eggs are not mine to touch, but the grey ones... my hands itch to touch them just once. Going by pure instinct, I run my hands across one of the eggs. The first shell burns a deep red, the grey slowly fading the longer I keep my palm there, as if I'm breathing life back into it.

I touch the others, and one by one each egg returns to its vibrant colour. The dragons growling and hissing above me instantly stop, and silence fills the cavern while I touch the eggs. I move from nest to nest, working my way through the many grey eggs, until the glow from all the brightly coloured shells makes it look like a rainbow has burst through the darkness.

The final egg bleeds into a brilliant gold, a different colour to all the others, and something tells me this one is special.

Out of nowhere, I gasp, nearly falling over as sharp pain lances through my stomach. Freyren swings her head towards me and roars loud enough to shake the very ground at my feet. I don't hear the shouting to begin with as I crawl through the water to my dragon. To my home now. We belong together and I never once thought there would be a chance I'd find my home in this world ever again. Everything has just changed.

"You need to ride!" Erax roars with nothing short of desperate panic in his voice. I let myself imagine for a second it is worry about me lurking in his tone. "Get into the sky! NOW!"

I can't ride a dragon alone! I can't make the words come out of my mouth while the pain is this bad. If I wasn't used to pain, I don't know how I would make my legs move. Erax is already in the water, running to me, when a red dragon lands in his path, blocking him. His shout echoes through the cavern. "Get on the fucking dragon before the bond kills you for not completing it! I nearly died at this moment you're in, and the longer you don't fly, the stronger the chance the bond will stop your heart!"

With every bit of strength and determination not to die that I have left, I get to my dragon's side. She is in pain, too. She lowers herself down for me, and I grab any scales, crawling myself to my feet even when my body screams for me to give up. To listen to the pain and just give up. Somehow, I climb up my dragon and onto her back, sitting wobbly in a smooth gap in the thorns on her back. She roars, but she doesn't move. "Fly!" I scream, but with horror lancing through my heart, I realise she doesn't understand me, and I don't speak her language. "Fuck. Fly, fly, fly. Please!"

"Not in that language!" Erax's voice barrels through the air. "*NIVAROSS*!"

I barely know how to pronounce it like he did, but I try, anyway. "Please, *nivaross*. Please."

How did Erax do this on his own for the first time? How did the king not die?

My king, my husband, is brave and I hate myself for loving that about him.

Freyren's clear eyes turn back and land on me. There is a sharpness in her gaze, a strength I've only ever seen in my own eyes in the mirror. We are both the last of our people, and we will not give up. We will rise together, and this world? It can be shattered into ice and remade after fire.

She slams through the waterfall, lashing me with water so strong that I nearly fall off. The air feels tight in my lungs as she flies up and up. I hold on tight to the scales in front of me, scales that feel like warm leather. The pain fades away as she flies straight up through the cavern, and by the time we kiss the skies, it's gone. The air is frosty up here, and immediately my fear of heights makes me scream. Freyren is gentle, letting me get used to her as we fly higher until we are going through the clouds. My stomach feels like it's made of jelly, but I lift my head, forcing myself to look while my ears ring and pop.

I can see the entire kingdom.

I'm left feeling stronger than ever as we glide into the open skies, nothing but sunlight and clouds for miles.

This is what it means to be free.

CHAPTER FIFTEEN

ERAX

My queen is a dragon rider.

Fuck, if I didn't desire her above all else before today, watching her claim and ride a dragon of her own has sealed it for me.

She is my end, wrapped in soft curves and rose gold hair.

With the others, we run outside to watch as my queen flies over the kingdom on her new dragon. Noble whistles. "A fucking ice blue dragon? None of the ice dragon eggs hatched before."

I grin. "Isn't she amazing?"

My other riders crowd round in shock as they watch the sky with me. Her dragon lets out a roar, a high-pitched one that reminds me of dolphins. Dragons in the cave, including mine, who stopped me from going to them earlier, roar back. I don't know what that means, but my queen is trouble. It's no shock to me her dragon would be too.

Adryn moves to Noble's side. He is an excellent rider and fucking lethal in battle, but he has a backwards view on women, which means we never fully get along. His family are all the same and see women as somehow less than us, or just things to own and have our kids. It's stupid because women are generally smarter and more capable than most of the men I know. If I had to pick someone to be a new rider, I would have picked my wife.

"Did she have a calling, Noble?" Adryn asks. "I'm not believing my eyes right now."

"If she did, she probably never under-stood it," Noble replies, glancing at me. "Why did you bring her here?"

I don't like the tone, but he is my best friend, my brother in every way but blood. It's been that way since we met as kids. Noble was the boy I took into the keep with me at thirteen and taught how to bond to a dragon even when my grandmother forbade it. I knew I needed an army of dragons to take The Drifting Kingdom and save everyone. At sixteen, he was at my side when we invaded; he had played his part as my spy well. "For the truth. And to let her see the eggs and dragons from a distance. The egg came to her and she took it. It reminded me of..."

I drift off, pushing down that memory. There are a few things I'm not proud of in my life, and that is one time. It is the worst of my memories of things I did to get the throne and make peace. All I ever wanted was to make a new world where dragons could live in peace with us, and I've done everything to get here. I push the memory away, like I always do, and focus on the skies. The curse, the assassins, they can fuck off for a moment.

Her dragon is huge, nearly as big as mine, but slenderer and quicker. I can't help but grin, like she can see me from down here. I'm so fucking proud of her. My wife is a fucking dragon rider. I always thought that we were not perfect for each other and that this was for the kingdom.

Then I kissed her, and she tasted like home. Mine. She is fucking mine.

When I fucked her for the first time? I knew no one was going to compare, and I was fucking done for. The more I get to know her, the more I believe that she has no idea what her parents were like, and I see how completely and utterly amazing she is for all she has survived. My cock is already growing hard from even thinking of fucking her again, and I carefully adjust myself before my trousers strangle me. Noble is watching the sky, his arms crossed, and he doesn't look happy. "Those dead eggs. She brought them back. How?"

"Maybe it is her gift," Babken says, moving closer. The bulky man crosses his arms, watching. He has always focused on logging the dragon gifts and working with the riders since he became one. "A rare gift she has been blessed with. I've not even heard of it in any of the dragon fables we have on record. How did she do it?"

"Who gives a shit? If she wasn't just

useful for opening her legs for the king, now she has the potential to make new riders." Adryn laughs, and I see red. Deep, blistering, crimson red. He doesn't even notice me move. "Heirs and dragons, what a good whore she—"

I punch his stupid fucking jaw to slam his mouth shut. Blood sprays as he rears back, and Noble grabs my shirt, pushing me away as Adryn crawls backwards with wide eyes. His jaw is broken, and his wails of pain are worth it.

"You might be one of my riders, but she is my queen! Disrespecting my queen is disrespecting me." I kick him back, forcing him to his knees. "Watch your fucking words or you will lose your tongue. You don't need it to ride in my army."

He stands and wisely walks away. I rub my knuckles as I turn back to watch my queen. It's not the first time I've punched Adryn over something dumb about women that has come out of his mouth. Noble is friends with him, and the only reason I haven't ended the bastard's life is because of that friendship and the fact he is one of my most skilled riders. Adryn should be more careful with my wife's name on my lips, especially when that wife is his queen and can heal dragon eggs. I will hopefully have more new riders soon to replace him.

We've lost far too many dragon eggs over the years to the grey, and we never knew what caused it. Perhaps Zepheira is right. Perhaps the dragons have never been the same since the attack and their grief carries to their womb. Ever since that attack, the dragons have let only me and Zepheira near their eggs. But they let Maelena; we all saw it and how she healed their dying eggs.

I'm glad she was already my wife when this new power came to the light of day. Our enemies would have made her a dragon-flying goddess princess to be saved if they found out. Now this will be seen as a blessing on our happy marriage and a gift from the gods themselves.

Noble speaks first and nothing really shuts him up, so it's no surprise he barely keeps quiet for a few minutes. I'm glad he stopped me from killing Adryn though as I might have done for saying a bad word against Maelena. "Ad is a prat, but he means she suddenly brought a great potential to bring our kingdom to a point where we are invincible and at peace. No one can stop you now. No one can stop us."

It's all I have wanted since I first climbed into that mountain. I found a dragon egg to bond with. I was fucking terrified as a teenager, but I had no choice that day. Ever since I was kid, I knew I was different to everyone else around me. I had powers, and I had to hide them from everyone but Noble. He had his own powers, his own dragon calling, and he listened when I told him the truth. We worked together to get our dragons. When I touched the egg for the first time, I knew that the dragon was mine and we would remake this world. A black egg hatched in my hands and, working on instinct alone, I took it into the water nearby as he exploded into a massive dragon who I thought might eat me. She didn't.

We flew instead. Once I was in the skies, I knew what I had to do with the power and knowledge I had. I knew I wouldn't be able to do it alone, and Noble didn't question me when I sent him for his dragon egg. In the years that passed as I planned my war, I collected riders from every village I could and followed every rumour of magic that I could hear. Every single teenager or man I found was happy to have an answer of why they had magic and what their destiny was. I never once found a woman with magic, and now I have.

I was always looking for her.

"The witches," Noble quickly hushes over their name as my blood runs colder than the ice dragon above. The curse will not touch my queen now, not when she is powerful and has a dragon. This is a protection even I cannot just give to her. "There are no mentions of a female rider. She could bring doom to us all."

Logic goes out of the window when superstitions whisper in the air.

"Women as riders are dangerous!" Zaal, one of my newer riders, shouts and several of them agree. The smart ones don't and move to the side, like they expect me to explode. Dragon riders' tempers are usually worse than a normal man's. A normal man doesn't have the fire of a dragon burning next to their soul. It doesn't just make them abnormal. It can make them dangerous.

I tilt my head to the side and let each one of them see the anger stirring in my eyes. I have done everything for them, for my kingdom, and the only person off limits to my riders is my wife. She is one of us now, and they will welcome her. Or I will make them.

"My wife can clearly ride a dragon that is bigger than yours and better than any of you have done before." I raise my tone. "When the queen comes back, you all better fucking bow to her and then go ask your females if they feel a need to come to the eggs."

When no one says anything, my anger rises.

Fucking morons.

My dragon riders are loyal to me, but their judgement needs to be readjusted. I should let my queen and her dragon freeze all their balls off, then we will see how much they like being male dragon riders.

When her dragon lands, my riders stay behind as I walk to her across the field as she slides down the dragon's wing, nearly falling over, but she stops herself. The dragon looks at me with enormous sea blue eyes, sniffing the air and snarling a little before going flying off into the sky, straight towards the cave to rest.

Tugging my cloak off, I go to wrap it around her, but she turns, looking up at me. Her pale cheeks are flushed from the cold air, but her eyes are wide with joy, and she is smiling. Fuck, she might as well knock my kneecaps out with that smile.

I'm surprised when she jumps into my arms, wrapping them tightly around my neck before she kisses me.

She fucking kissed me.

I groan as pleasure surges in my balls, and I want nothing more than to rip her clothes off and fuck her in front of everyone here until she is dripping with me. The kiss is short and sweet like her, but it's the first time she's kissed me. Blood rushes straight away from my head to my cock within seconds before she breaks away.

Maelena steps back and blinks a few times, her awareness sinking in, bringing that delightful coyness that makes my cock hard. "I'm—I'm sorry, I—"

I grab her neck, tilting her head back. "Don't you ever apologise for kissing me. I'm your husband. You never need to apologise for kissing me or doing anything to me except trying to kill me, perhaps."

Her eyes sparkle with that same old defiance. Fuck, I love that look.

"I'm not apologising for that."

"Really?" I cock an eyebrow. I wrap the cloak around her shoulders and pick her up, making her gasp. She holds onto me as I carry her back to the castle, and I expect a fight, but it doesn't come. She lets me carry her. "You must be tired or in shock if you're letting me carry you. You're the first female dragon rider in history, Maelena. Congratulations."

"Fighting you is tiring. Just for now, I'm going to let you. Then you can show me the truth."

She swallows a yawn and my eyes flicker to her lips. I want to taste her again, but she is exhausted and sleep will claim her soon enough. I need to be holding her when it does. I set her down on the bed in our room, and she curls up at my side, yawning once before falling into a deep sleep.

I watch my wife, the first female dragon rider, and wonder if there will ever be a time she won't hate me for what I did to get us here.

CHAPTER SIXTEEN

I settle into the bathtub, letting the warm water lap over my body. Breathing in the fragrant steam, I rest my head against the metallic tub and close my eyes. In all the years I spent in captivity, a hot bath was one of the things I often fantasised about. Back then, it seemed so far out of my reach. The cold-water basins, often frozen in winter, and the cheap soap were all I ever got to clean myself. Sometimes I was given an old sponge, and I remember feeling like I'd been handed a pot of gold.

But this—this beautiful, luxurious bath that can be drawn at my command—is unlike what I could have imagined. After riding my very own dragon, and then Erax, my aching bones have needed this. I sink down until my hair floats around me.

Through my bond, I can feel Freyren at rest, exhausted after her first time flying. It blows my mind to think she was only born a few hours ago. Although the magic allowed her to grow, she still has a lot of maturing to do and heaps more growing according to Zepheira. That worries me since she already looks bigger than some of the other dragons.

Just how big will my dragon grow?

A knock on the door startles me. "Yes?"

No response.

"Erax?"

If it is Erax, he's determined to make me drag myself out of this lovely bath.

"Gods above!" I grumble under my breath as I stand in the water and reach for my bathrobe. I wrap it around my body, pulling the tie tight. He's lucky I got to enjoy my bath for a good fifteen minutes before he returned. Why is he back so soon anyway? Now that our honeymoon period is officially over, he said he had several duties to tend to, and he told me to spend the rest of my day resting. I was just beginning to feel rested.

"I hope you come bearing food. I'm so hungry I could eat a dragon."

I squeeze my hair with another towel and make my way to the bathroom door.

The towel slips through my fingers when I open it and see who's on the other side.

It's not Erax. It's not even a servant. It's—

"Lochlan!"

I leap into his arms. He catches me, my wet face pressing against his gold chestplate. The same armour the guards wear.

"Why are you dressed as a guard?" I ask, looking up at him.

Lochlan pulls away but keeps his hands on my arms. "It was the only way I could get in." That familiar lopsided grin stretches over his face. "Missed me?"

My eyes well with tears.

"Loch, you have no idea how much I've missed you. There's *so* much I need to tell you!" And ask him. Why did he go back? Is Noble truly his brother? My reflection gleams at me from his armour, making me pause. This isn't just any armour. It's the king's guard armour. "How did you get this?"

"Dasinth. He brought it with him after the feast and asked me to bring you this.

Seems after all these years, he's had a change of heart."

I look down at the sealed envelope in his hands. "A letter?"

My uncle has never written to me. I wonder what he wrote that he couldn't have said in person. Before I take the letter from him, I look up at Lochlan. His face looks tired, and in the time we've been separated, it's like he's aged several years. I can't imagine any of this has been easy on him either. Sister Gabriella probably put him through hell when I left.

"Did they hurt you?" I whisper, a familiar pain clenching my stomach.

He shakes his head. "Don't worry about me. Now open the letter."

Giving him the side-eye, I decide to do as he says. I want to know what's inside too. I slide my nail under the wax to break the seal and pull out the contents.

"It isn't a letter," I say, withdrawing a small painting. My eyes sting again. "It's a portrait—of my parents."

With the words *Do not forget* written under them in my uncle's hand. The corners of the painting remain blackened, scorched from the fire that ravaged our home. They're so young in this portrait. So happy. The tears that slip from my eyes splash my mother's face and my father's chest. I don't recall them ever smiling like this. It must have been painted before I was born. I turn the painting around, checking if my uncle has written anything else, but only those three words remain.

"Do not forget…" I turn to Lochlan. "What do you think it means?"

I tuck the painting into my robe. It's not like I could ever forget my parents. Or what Erax did to them.

"I think Dasinth wants you to remember there are still people loyal to your family," he replies, "and that you're not alone in this." He then reaches out to gently wipe a strand of wet hair from my temple, cupping my chin with his other hand. "You never were alone, Lena."

The muscles in my chest tighten. Something about the way Lochlan is looking at me feels strange. For the first time in my life, his touch makes me want to pull away. The door is still open, and if someone sees us... I shudder to think what Erax would do.

Through our bond, my dragon bristles, also feeling uneasy.

Mine. Erax's words invade my mind all over again. *You're mine.*

"Loch—"

My words are stolen as Lochlan's mouth crashes upon my own. His lips press firmly against mine as his hands twist through my hair, pulling me back to him. I tense my body, but I don't fight him. In my shock and confusion, I let him pull me in, and for the briefest of moments, I close my eyes, neither willing nor reluctant to return his kiss.

I would be lying if I said I never wondered what it would be like to kiss Lochlan.

Lochlan, the boy who eased my suffering at the convent with his kindness. Lochlan, who grew into the man that tried to help me escape and win my freedom from the cage that bound us. Once or twice, I wondered what his lips would feel like against mine and if my heart would beat so loud it would erupt from my chest. As his tongue slips past my lips, my heart doesn't beat.

It sinks.

This kiss doesn't just feel strange. It feels wrong.

I push my hands against his armour, but Lochlan's grip tightens, his fingers digging into my arms. Then all of a sudden, he stops, and in his shadow stands Erax watching us. His body seems to swallow up the entire doorway as he stands there.

Panic flares through me and I step back quickly. "Erax, this isn't what you think."

Erax says nothing and keeps his eyes on Lochlan. The fact he says nothing scares me more than if he did speak. I know Erax is possessive of me, not only because I'm his wife but because I'm his queen too. And he just found his queen kissing another man.

"This is my friend Lochlan," I say quickly as my body starts to shake.

Erax sweeps into the room with quick, heavy strides. "Then by all means, continue as you were with your *friend*. Don't let me stop you." He drops into the armchair by the dresser and grips the armrests, raising his leg over his right knee. "I'm really fucking curious to see how this plays out."

His eyes latch onto me while Lochlan glares at him. He doesn't bow or even acknowledge him as his king. He sizes Erax up like a predator would their prey. All the while, Erax looks at me like I'm about to be devoured by him.

"Go on." He gives a quick, dismissive wave of his hand. "You have about three minutes before my guards drag that little fucker down to my keep."

"Your Majes—"

Erax cuts Lochlan off with a single look. Just a look, a mere tilt of his head, and any words that needed to be said are conveyed with deafening profoundness. Erax wants blood.

Lochlan's eyes flick down to the floor, and I'm suddenly reminded of the boy I knew at the convent, the quiet, submissive Lochlan who paled in Sister Gabriella's presence. Reality is sinking in for the both of us now.

I touch his arm gently and try to pull him behind me. Erax zeroes in on the placement of my hand, and his gaze darkens. In the blink of an eye, he's barrelling into Lochlan, tackling him to the ground. I'm knocked to the side, my hip banging into the side of the dresser, while Erax's fist repeatedly slams down into Lochlan's face.

Everything happens so fast I'm barely able to plead with him to stop.

I try to manoeuvre myself between them, but the guards charging into the room hold me back. I'm forced to watch as Erax beats Lochlan to a pulp. He doesn't fight back. He just lies there, taking hit after hit, his fate sealed.

"Please, Erax!" I sob his name out, trying to twist myself free of the guards. "Let him go. Please, just let him go!"

Erax only lets Lochlan go once he's lost consciousness. Panting heavily, he stands and looks at me. His face is splashed with Lochlan's blood, and the crazed look in his eyes is unlike anything I have seen in a human before. It's feral. Animalistic.

"Take him to the keep," he orders, stepping over Lochlan's body, "and get your hands off my wife."

His guards release me. Quickly they

follow his orders: they drag Lochlan to his feet and haul him from the room. I hear him groan, though I barely see Lochlan through the tears clouding my vision. I caused this. If I had pulled away from him sooner, Erax might never have seen, and none of this would have happened. This is all my fault.

For a painfully long moment, the room is quiet. Erax thrusts open the drink cabinet by the window and pulls out a half-empty bottle. He knocks back several mouthfuls and then breathes a sigh, as if he's just finished a long day tending his royal duties. As if he hadn't just nearly beaten my friend to death.

I let my tears fall, letting the pain behind them turn into anger.

"He was my friend."

"He's a traitor," Erax spits. "And, if I'm not mistaken, he's the *friend* who tried to help you escape."

"Tried to free me, yes."

I immediately regret saying that. Erax is already intent on killing, and I just handed him a knife with those words. He glares at me.

"Free you?" He scoffs, then, in one impossibly swift movement, pushes me up against the wall. His huge body pins me underneath him, and his face comes within inches of mine, his breath fanning my cheeks. Slowly he runs his knuckles down my cheek, stained with Lochlan's blood. "What about now, Mist? Do you still long for freedom?" His hand falls between my legs, and I gasp when he caresses me. A cruel smile works its way over his lips. "You certainly didn't last night when I made you come so hard you screamed my name."

"Erax, stop—"

"Oh, I'm just getting started, and it seems, my beautiful wife, so are you."

His smile grows wider when I suddenly moan. I try to close my legs, but Erax forces them open with his knee. I've never seen him so angry—his eyes so dark and hateful and yet beautiful at the same time. It frightens me. It also makes my body shiver against him as unbidden desire rises through me.

"In the old days, the king would have your head for what you just did," Erax whispers. "Or lock you in a dungeon and let you rot there for the rest of your life."

His fingers gently caress me, teasing and gliding over my sensitive area. His smile grows even wider and cruel when he pushes inside and takes in how wet I am. I can't help it, and we both know deep down I don't want to. "I could feed you to my dragon for treason," he breathes, "and our entire kingdom would watch." He eases his fingers in and out, his eyes never leaving me. "But I'd rather feed your friend to her and make you watch as I fuck you in front of them."

"Please..." I gasp out another moan as he rubs my sensitive spot with his thumb. "Just stop, Erax!"

He stops. As if the darkness with him is melting away, Erax withdraws his hand and pulls away from between my legs. He keeps his other hand on my wrists pinned above my head though, and when he leans in, his eyes are still incinerating.

"Don't *ever*... do that again."

"It wasn't what you—"

"Ever," he growls, grabbing my throat, "again. Or so help me, Maelena, I will burn every man who looks at you. Do you understand?"

His dilated pupils reflect my image back to me, and I'm surrounded by flames that swirl in his eyes. His dragon is just as angry and possessive as him. I didn't mean for any of this to happen. I certainly didn't mean for Lochlan to kiss me. Although it felt so wrong when he did, like kissing a brother. It felt nothing like when I kiss Erax, and my soul feels like it's on fire.

I nod at him, unable to breathe let alone speak.

"Good." Erax lets me go. "Now if your *friend* would like to keep his head, he better not come back here, or I'll rip it off with my bare fucking hands. Is that understood?"

Again, I nod, my body still trembling from the fear and desire he wrought upon me. Erax pulls away. He adjusts his clothes, sweeps a hand through his hair, then he turns and makes for the door.

"Where are you going?" I whisper, even though I know the answer.

The fact Erax doesn't reply confirms it. He's going to the keep.

As he slams the door behind him, I reach into my pocket. My hands shaking, I hold the picture of my parents as more tears splash their faces, this time for different reasons. No, I will not forget. Just like I won't forget all the terrible things Erax has done since he burned my world to ash.

I will never forgive him, but I hate the way my legs beg me to go after my king.

CHAPTER SEVENTEEN

I don't know how long I've cried, but I know I haven't gone out of bed since Erax left. I know that the tears won't stop, and I feel like I'm absolutely drowning, completely and utterly drowning. I cling to the pillow tightly as my swollen eyes sting from how much I've cried. But I don't dare even lift my head. He's going to kill Loch, and it's all my fault.

A single kiss is a death sentence, and I should have stopped it.

I should have done something— anything.

I didn't even know Loch had feelings for me. It took me by surprise. Erax didn't even give me a chance to explain, but part of me doesn't blame him for his reaction. I am his queen at the end of the day.

I never wanted to be queen, let alone his, yet here I am, and I'm alone.

My bedroom door opens, but I don't bother raising my head from the pillow, knowing it's probably the maid coming to check on me again. To try to coax me out of bed and help calm me down with more offers of spiced teas.

When the smell of fire and roses washes over me, I lift my head a little to meet the king's gaze. He looks broken, and it crushes me that I did this to him too. His riding leathers are gone, and he's wearing a black shirt that's open at the top and tucked into black trousers, but it's not his clothes that scream broken to me. It's his expression on his face, the hurt in his beautiful eyes, that I've never seen before. It's almost like the fire that burned in him is slowly going out, and I know in my heart I don't want to see those flames die.

This bond between us has changed everything so quickly, and I can't lie to myself that I hate him. It's not as simple as that anymore. Even when I want to hate Erax, completely despise him with every ounce of my soul, I can't deny my feelings for him. I will never forget or forgive him for what he did, but my heart has been split and its broken pieces are crying for him.

"Erax..."

"Fuck you," he snarls at me. "Hating you? That was so fucking easy. So easy, right before I saw you." He lets out a hollow laugh. "Before I saw you, I swore to the gods that I would always hate you. I hated everything you were for what your parents did to this world. The monsters that they were. For all of it."

"What are you talk—"

"Don't interrupt me!" He grits his teeth, and his eyes flash with flames again. "Just for once, don't." I bite my tongue and nod once since it's all I can do. "Then I saw you. Saw you on that stupid fucking cart, dressed in rags. Fuck... Everything changed. I don't know what I was expecting you to be like. I really didn't. I thought it'd be a chore to marry you. I thought I'd hate it. As much as I hate what lies in your blood. But when I met you, when I saw you for the first time, every-thing changed. I wanted you. You were so beautiful and enchanting... and fuck, I wanted you more than I ever wanted my dragon to be mine."

I can't breathe. Erax has never opened up like this before.

"If we met at random and you weren't the princess and I weren't the king, I would have still wanted you and said fuck it all. I would want you in any world, in any place, with any title, because something in here"—he slams a closed fist over his heart—"tells me that you are mine. So, fuck you for making me want you, Maelena. Fuck you for letting me be inside you and know that nothing and no one is ever going to compare. And really, truly, fuck you for making me have feelings for you that made me want to die when I saw you kiss another man. Fuck you for making me love you, Maelena."

His words knock the air from my lungs. My chest tightens and aches, and I feel like I'm about to pass out. I stare at this traitor king who is every bit mine as I am his. I want to scream at him. To pull myself out from this bed and make him see how much he's torn me to pieces.

"It meant nothing," I whisper instead. "Lochlan has never kissed me before, and I was trying to stop it even before you came in. Loch... he's my friend, and that's it."

For once, Erax deserves the truth from me too.

"I had a crush on him as a girl, I guess, because he helped me in the convent. He was the only one who helped me. He looked after me when I was whipped. But he never took it further, and it was just that—a crush. A stupid, silly little crush that died out through the years, and he became like a brother to me. I realised that when he kissed me. It didn't have any lust or desire, or that burning feeling in my chest that I seem to feel only when I look at you. So, fuck you right back, Erax, for making me fall in love with you too."

Erax falls to his knees. He looks like he's in pain or just completely dumbfounded. Whatever the reason, it makes me get out of the bed and fall down beside him. I take his head between my hands, our faces inches apart.

"I know I should hate you for what you

did. I should hate you for everything that you are, but I don't. And I'm not sure who I hate more for that—myself or whichever cruel god decided our marriage was destined to be this real."

My voice breaks as he reaches for me. His hand wraps around my waist, tugging me against him. I sink my face into his neck, breathing in the scent I despised but have grown to yearn for. There is no point denying this anymore.

I'm in love with Erax, and as he holds me in his arms, I know he's in love with me too. It's the biggest fuck you in history.

He smells my hair, speaking softly to me. "I don't hate the gods for this. I will treasure them forever for bringing you to me. We're perfect for each other. I will tell you every truth and the reasons why." I peer up at him through my lashes. "I'm not a good person, Maelena. I've done many things I've lived to regret. But what I did that day—it was for justice and peace, and I won't ever regret bringing my people that."

He picks me up and throws me on the bed, covering me with his huge body, and I believe him. I want to know the truth and the reason behind it all, because I've gotten to know Erax and see that he is more than his violent past. His hand digs into my hair as he kisses me, his tongue deeply sinking into my mouth, and I gasp at the invasion. Lochlan's kiss is almost laughable compared to how it feels to have Erax kiss me now, and my body knows it.

We burn for one male.

One king.

Erax is my husband, and I want him. I'm done fighting it. I know my parents will hate me for giving in to him. Maybe I'm just as much of a traitor as he is.

I tug at his shirt, breaking all the buttons as his hands run down my night-dress, yanking it down so my breasts are exposed to the cold air. He groans as he cups one of them, rubbing his thumb softly over my nipple, and a grin spreads over his lips.

"Is my queen wet for me?"

I nod and he grips my throat, making me look at him. His eyes are shifting into a darker green, narrowing in a way that reminds me of his dragon. "Were you wet for him?"

Embarrassment floods me. "No," I breathe out. "Only you."

"Let me see," he murmurs, sinking down my body, and I love the pleased tone in his voice. He pushes up my nightdress so it wraps around my waist, and I'm bared fully to him. A blush burns my cheeks as he parts my legs, and a growl echoes from him. "Fuck, you're dripping, and I haven't even touched you yet." He presses his lips against me, softly breathing over my sensitive spot. "I want you all over my face, and then I want you to kiss me as you ride your king."

I grin at him. He usually takes control, but any way he is inside me sounds perfect to me right now. I wriggle on the bed.

"Yes, Erax... please."

"I like when you beg," he murmurs against my skin, kissing me once on the soft, delicate skin of my inner thigh. He doesn't make me wait any longer before he devours me like the dragon he is. His hot tongue parts my folds so quickly, licking all the way up my slit to my clit and swirling around the spot there as I moan and cry out in pleasure. He is relentless, taking every moan and scream like they are personal treasures for him to hoard, and he knows exactly how to make me explode under his touch.

Pleasure destroys me within minutes, crashing down on my body before spreading across every inch of me. I fall back onto the bed, my body twitching and shaking as I come down from the high.

Erax looks utterly pleased with himself as he rises up. He wipes his hand across his wet mouth and then reaches for his trousers. I part my legs and wait breathlessly for the best part. He only gets one button undone before there's a knock on the door, and we both pause.

Erax snarls and his eyes darken with a murderous look. "I don't care who the fuck it is, go away or I'll fucking kill you!"

Noble's voice echoes back. "I'm coming in there whether you want me to or not. It's an emergency, so stop fucking her."

Erax grits his teeth and fastens his button again. He picks me up softly, but there's still that dark, murderous look on his face. I give him a smile. We don't need to rush. We can continue on and on, and he knows it.

"I'm going to kill him."

I rush to the wardrobe, tugging on a green tunic and a pair of grey leggings. Erax watches me while pacing by the window, trying to calm himself down. "He's your best friend."

"Still going to kill him because I know he heard you come, and that delicious sound is just for me."

Erax stops pacing and grabs me, pulling me in for a long, slow kiss where I can taste myself on his lips. Then he moves back and, without looking at the door, shouts for Noble to come in. Noble enters quickly, and for the first time ever, he doesn't bow to his king. He's wearing heavy red armour that carries my parents' distinctive crest on the breastplate and a gold cloak.

My eyes widen when I see he has a strange glowing crossbow in his hand. He doesn't even pause before he lifts it and shoots six arrows straight into Erax's chest. The impact sends Erax flying across the room from my side, his blood spraying my chest and face.

I freeze in shock, and my bond to my dragon causes her feelings of shock to amplify them. She is losing it in the keep. She wants to keep me safe and our husband too. That familiar icy feeling sweeps over me, and I know it's my power about to unleash itself. I let it come forward, but then it suddenly vanishes when an arrow pierces my arm.

I try to scream but no sound makes its way past my vocal cords. As if dazed, I watch in pure horror as three more arrows are shot into Erax, each one of them glowing and radiating a strange black essence. It's magic. Dark magic. They must be subduing me while killing Erax.

My shock wears off and my scream finally tears its way out of me. Six arrows hold Erax in place, pinned against the wall. Blood pours heavily from each wound. Stumbling, I manage to drag myself to my feet and run over to Erax, sickness rising in my throat. Noble catches me around the waist before I reach him. He twists the arrow deeper into my arm and laughs in my ear.

"Too much has been done for you to start growing feelings for him now. Remember The Drifting Kingdom, Maelena? Because it hasn't forgotten you."

I twist in his arms, screaming at him. "You betraying bastard! Let me go!" My voice breaks as my cries turn into sobs. "You were his best friend! A rider! How could you?!"

He laughs again, this time in my face, as his hand cups my ass and pulls me against him. A disgusted shudder runs through me. "He will die soon enough. The arrows were a gift from the witches. They promised he'll die and so will his dragon. Don't worry about him following us. You're free and hopefully you have a nice heir in that stomach of yours we can use. You will be far more powerful than you already are with a babe in there." He turns my head, forcing me to look him in the eye. "Don't you remember who I really am? I was there the night he killed your parents." I go still in his arms, and he leans in. "Your father had just betrothed us the week before, and the night of the attack, I offered you my help but you would not listen." I remember the boy in the corridor, but his hair was brown... or was it ash? Could he have been blond? "I couldn't get to you until now, and it's a shame he ruined you, but I'll take you, anyway."

Horror sinks into my chest. "Who the fuck are you?"

A leering look contorts his face. "You're about to find out."

I start to scream, crawling my way out of his arms to try to get back to Erax. Lochlan steps into the room in front of us, his eyes wide as he comes up to me. He looks as terrible as the last time I saw him, but he apparently wasn't beaten that badly if he can help Noble kidnap me and kill a king. My horror turns into betrayal, and my screams turn into sobbing pleas.

"Nooo!" I scream out as if Lochlan just stabbed me in the chest and ripped out my heart. "Don't tell me you're part of this. Not you, please!"

But I know just from the look on his face that Lochlan is part of this. He was part of it all along.

"Just forget him, Lena. He's nothing."

Lochlan is nothing to me now.

He looks over at his brother. "Knock her out. It will be easier to get her out of the castle if she is silent."

"NOOO! Loch, please save Erax! Don't do th—"

Something hard slams into the back of my head, and in the darkness, all I can smell is fire and roses. All I can do is beg the gods to save my king...

To be continued in book two: A BOND OF ICE AND GLASS.

Preorder here!

G. BAILEY

G. BAILEY IS A USA TODAY AND INTERNATIONAL
BESTSELLING AUTHOR OF FANTASY AND
PARANORMAL ROMANCE.
SHE LIVES IN ENGLAND WITH HER CHEEKY
CHILDREN, HER GORGEOUS (AND SLIGHTLY MAD)
GOLDEN RETRIEVERS AND HER TEENAGE
SWEETHEART TURNED HUSBAND.

HTTPS://WWW.GBAILEYAUTHOR.COM/

BOOKS BY THIS AUTHOR:

HER GUARDIANS SERIES
HER FATE SERIES
PROTECTED BY DRAGONS SERIES
LOST TIME ACADEMY SERIES
THE DEMON ACADEMY SERIES
DARK ANGEL ACADEMY SERIES
SHADOWBORN ACADEMY SERIES
FALL MOUNTAIN SHIFTERS SERIES

THE REJECTED MATE SERIES

THE EVERLASTING CURSE SERIES

ROYAL REAPER ACADEMY SERIES

DARK FAE PARANORMAL PRISON SERIES

SAVED BY PIRATES SERIES

THE MARKED SERIES

THE ALPHA BROTHERS SERIES

A DEMON'S FALL SERIES

THE FAMILIAR EMPIRE SERIES

FROM THE STARS SERIES

THE FOREST PACK SERIES

THE SECRET GODS PRISON SERIES

THE DRAGON CROWN SERIES

THE WYERN CLAN SERIES

CONSEQUENCE.

OTHER PEN NAMES:

LOUISE ROSE & VIVIAN STAR.

SCARLETT SNOW

USA Today Bestselling Author Scarlett Snow lives in Scotland with her family and writes under various pen names, so whether you're in the mood for Paranormal, Fantasy, Sci-Fi, Reverse Harem, or M/M romance, Scarlett has got you covered!

You can join her newsletter here for exclusive updates & freebies: www.wintersnowpub-lishing.com/newsletter

BOOKS BY THIS AUTHOR:
PREDATORS & PREY SERIES
SHADOWBORN ACADEMY SERIES
SHADOWBORN PRISON SERIES
THE REJECTED MATE SERIES
CONSEQUENCE
EVERAFTER ACADEMY SERIES
BEAUTY'S WOLVES
GRIMM

SAPHYRE

THE QUEEN'S PROTECTORS

GHOULS

VILLAINOUS HEARTS

VILLAINOUS SOULS

OTHER PEN NAMES:

KYRA SNOW. KATZE SNOW. NORA
WINTERS.

SHADOWBORN ACADEMY BONUS READ...

CHAPTER ONE

The moonlight bleeding through the trees create flickering shadows that dance around me. I should be afraid of them like all the other children are, but I'm not. These shadows are safe. They're not like the ones watching me from the treetops, waiting to snatch me off the ground.

No, these shadows are different.

They're my friends.

The faeries hiding in them follow me like they always do when I come into the Enchanted Forest. I can't see them but I can hear them giggling and whispering in my ear. They flick my dark curly hair over my shoulders and play with the ribbons on my light blue dress, then the frills of my white socks with the little bunny rabbits on them. It's their way of saying hello and it makes me giggle as I skip through the forest, humming to the song Mama always sings to me before I go to sleep.

Mama and Papa warned me not to follow these faeries. They said they're not like the rest and I'll be in deep trouble if I ever go out to play after dark. That's when the faeries come out. They sing to children like me and promise us things beyond our wildest dreams, but nobody ever sees them again once they follow the faeries into the forest. Mama said it's because they gobble them up for supper. I don't believe her. I mean, how horrible would that be? I don't think we taste very nice.

Pitch said the real reason the children don't come back is magical.

He told me that they grow wings and go to live with the faeries. He said I can do that, too, once I make my wish. I'm so excited. I can hear him singing to me and I start humming along to his favourite song, the one about the raven and the wishing well. I follow his voice, excited to play with him again and eat snacks and tell each other stories. No one else can see or hear Pitch apart from me and the faeries. Although we're the same age, he doesn't look like any of the boys from my village. He's extremely pale with glowing amber eyes and long ebony hair that sways around him like the shadows do in here. I know he's different and that's why I like him.

That's why I'm following him.

Now that it's my eighth birthday, Pitch is going to let me make a wish in the well he sings about. He says only special humans—the chosen ones—get to make a wish here. Sometimes he says funny things like that and I don't understand him. All I want is a pair of shiny blue shoes, the same ones as my dolly. Pitch says the faeries are going to give me them and then I'll finally have the same outfit as my little dolly.

The faeries guide me to the edge of a clearing which is bright from the moonlight shining down. I wave goodbye to them, even though I can't see where they are, then I continue humming and skipping after Pitch.

I can see him now, sitting on top of the well, and my heart soars as I race through the clearing. Once I reach the well, he lifts me onto the stone with him. It's wide enough that the two of us can stand together without falling into the hole.

"It's time to make your wish," he says, and my stomach fills with butterflies. "Are you ready to be born again?" I don't know what he means by that; I just want the lovely shoes. I nod anyway, and Pitch smiles at me. "Then close your eyes."

When I do this, I hold my breath, too excited to breathe.

My heart feels like it's going to burst out from my chest. I feel dizzy and sick and excited.

"Do you remember what we talked about?" Pitch asks quietly. "What you do once you make your wish? It's very important that you don't forget that part."

"I won't forget," I tell him firmly, peeking through my eyelashes. "Can I say it now? Can I make my wish?"

He giggles and lets go of my hand. "Go on, Corvina. Make your wish and make it count."

I let out an excited squeal, then I scrunch up my little face and think really hard because I don't want to mess this up.

—Hello faeries! Please can I have the same shoes as my dolly? You know, the sparkly blue

shoes with the pretty bows on the silver buckles? I would like them very much. Thank you.—

With my wish uttered, I open my eyes. Pitch is gone just like he said he would be and I'm alone on the well. I look down into the tunnel of darkness stretching before me. A loose pebble falls away from the edge and drops into the well. It takes forever to splash through the water at the bottom, and I gulp, my palms turning sweaty against my dress.

For my wish to come true, I need to go down there.

Pitch said he'll be waiting for me and that the faeries will even give me wings so that I don't hurt myself. I'll be just like the other children who followed the faeries into the woods and lived happily ever after. Maybe I'll even be able to see my friends, Bella, and Michael and Agnes.

We'll all be faeries together, like we used to talk about.

I turn around and spread my arms out like wings, smiling at the thought of seeing my friends from school again. Taking a deep breath and holding it in my chest, I close my eyes and fall down into the well, praying that Mama and Papa were wrong about the faeries, and about Pitch, the monster hiding under my bed...

Before I plunge to my death, I wake up with a gasp for air, crutching my thin bedsheets in my hands. Pitch wasn't waiting for me. There was nothing but pain and misery at the bottom of that stupid well and my innocent ass didn't know any better back then.

I fell into magical darkness, and as everyone here tells me, that's when I became a shadowborn.

But that's not the part that haunts me every night in my dreams. Oh, no. It's what happened after the pain and misery—after I drowned in all the magical water, my eight-year-old body absorbing it like it was sugar and I was a starving kid. When my heart started beating again and I opened my eyes, I lay floating on my back as the moon drew closer and closer to me. I remember crying and thinking I had been turned into a bug instead of a faery, but it was just the water healing my shattered bones and floating me up to the surface.

The second my feet touched the earth

again, my power exploded and I destroyed everything in a five-mile radius, including all the people in the houses.

Including my parents.

And the only living thing was me, covered in ash, lying on the forest floor as the sun rose into a blood-red sky.

Talk about a birthday to remember.

After that, I was picked up by the Shadow Wardens, protectors of the magical world, and thrown in a shadowborn foster home with all the other children that are like me. Only they didn't kill hundreds of people and not one of them in here see their powers like the curse it really is.

"You having those dreams again?" Sage asks, sitting up on her bed next to me and staring at me, the moonlight highlighting her beige skin, curly pink hair that isn't at all messy even though she just woke up. Sage Millhouse is the only bit of this foster home that I've ever cared about and I'm certain it's the same way for her. We came here on the same day, two scared kids who wanted nothing more than to escape this hellhole and the new powers we have. Sage got her power the way most of the kids here did, by being bitten by a shadowborn in their animal state. One bite is enough to infuse any soul with shadow magic, and all it took for Sage was a bite from a fox in her garden.

The fox was never seen again, and Sage nearly died, only to survive and be taken from her parents to come and live here.

The foster home is full of those stories, and it's the main reason I don't talk about my past.

"Always."

It's all I need to say for Sage to get off her bed and head out of the room. I follow her, the old wooden floorboards creaking under my barefeet with each step. Sage holds the timber door open and we head outside into the garden. The cool air is refreshing for only a second before it's nothing but cold nipping at my skin.

"Ready?" I ask her as I stare up, the darkness and shadows comforting me like they always do.

Sage doesn't reply, though I'm unsurprised as she isn't one for words. That's why I like her. I watch her bright purple eyes as she disappears in a cloud of black smoke. The darkness. It's become a blanket of sorts to people like us. As the blackness fades away, there is nothing more than a hawk sitting on the ground, its lavender eyes staring up at me. I grin as I close my own silver eyes and do the next best thing in the world.

I let the darkness take me, creating me into something more.

Something so much better than I already am.

My body disappears into the darkness but my mind always stays, loving the comfort as I shift into a raven and follow Sage into the skies of Blackpool.

Read more here...

Printed in Great Britain
by Amazon